Legends & Lore

Ireland's Folk Tales

MICHAEL SCOTT

Delacorte Press

Text copyright © 2021 by Michael Scott
Jacket art copyright © 2021 by Shane Rebenschied

All rights reserved. Published in the United States by
Delacorte Press, an imprint of Random House Children's Books,
a division of Penguin Random House LLC, New York.

Delacorte Press is a registered trademark and the colophon is a
trademark of Penguin Random House LLC.

Visit us on the Web! rhcbooks.com

Educators and librarians, for a variety of teaching tools,
visit us at RHTeachersLibrarians.com

Library of Congress Cataloging-in-Publication Data
is available upon request.
ISBN 978-0-593-38176-2 (hc) — ISBN 978-0-593-38178-6 (lib. bdg.) —
ISBN 978-0-593-38179-3 (ebook)

The text of this book is set in 11.5-point Sabon.
Interior design by Jen Valero

Printed in Canada
10 9 8 7 6 5 4 3 2 1
First Edition

ONE MORE FOR PIERS

Contents

Introduction

When people think of Irish folklore, usually the first creature who comes to mind is the Leprechaun. They're sure to know about the banshee, the fairy woman, who sings to warn of a death in the family, and St. Patrick is always mentioned. But that's probably all they know.

While everyone is familiar with the Egyptian, Greek, and Roman gods, few can name any of the Irish gods and goddesses—Danu and the Dagda, Banba, or even Manannan, Lord of the Sea.

Everyone knows about the kraken, the gorgon, or the minotaur, but outside the Celtic Isles, few know about the serpent Oilliphéist, the fear gorta, the walking dead, the dullahan, the headless horseman, or the merrow, the underwater people who have feet instead of fish tails.

Where other cultures went into the Underground, the Irish went to the Otherworld, and there were different types of otherworlds: the paradise, Mag Mell; Tir na nOg, the land of the young; Tir fo Thuinn, the land beneath the waves. There were fairy mounds in the earth and floating islands off the coast and in the middle of lakes.

The Irish stories survived intact because the country was never invaded by the Greeks or Romans and because Ireland has its own native language, Irish. It is a most beautiful and expressive language: *banshee* comes from *bean-sidhe,* which means "fairy woman." The skeletal *fear ghorta* is "the man of hunger," and Oilliphéist comes from "great worm." Translate place names from English into Irish and you can begin to see the history of the place: *Dublin* comes from *Dubh Linn,* "the black pool," around which the original town was built. *Derry* was originally *doire,* which means "a grove of oaks;" *Belfast* comes from *beal,* meaning "mouth," because it is at the mouth of a river. *Gallimh,* which means "stony," became *Galway.*

Wrapped in this language are the most incredible stories, which I've been collecting for many years. Here are just a few of my favorites.

Legends & Lore

King of the Leprechauns

One cold, bitter night—when the stars were hard and sharp and brilliant, spelling out their patterns across the skies—the Small Folk came to the land of Erin in the metal ships of the Tuatha De Danann. As humans measure time, that was many thousands of years ago, though the Small Folk are long-lived and so it may seem like less time to them. This is the story of their coming, and of the next great king of the leprechauns . . .

The leprechauns came to the tiny island that would one day become the land of Erin when the world was young. They had traveled across the vast western sea from the land of the De Danann folk, which they had been forced to flee when the ground started shifting and moving. In a single night, the mountains had spat fire and churning mud had burst up from the sea bed; the seas had risen and the waters had turned to boiling. Many of the De Danann folk believed that they had angered their terrible goddess, the Lady Danu, but no one knew how or why.

The Small Folk, who knew the ways of the wind and waves, the patterns of the earth and rivers, knew that the island of the De Danann was threatened with destruction. And so, while others huddled in their cellars and temples, praying to their goddess, the leprechauns had loaded up the huge metal ships with goods and tools, with sacks of grain, dried meat, and hard bread, with healing herbs and the seeds of rare trees and bushes, and a few of the ancient books and charts of the De Danann. And they sailed away just in time.

On the morning of the fifth day since they had sailed from the isle of the De Danann, Niall, the king of the leprechauns, called his sons together. The king was the oldest of the Small Folk—some even said he was the oldest creature in the world, that he had walked the world in the time of the dragons, before the first humans had appeared. He was taller than most of the Small Folk; his back was straight, his hair and beard were snow white, and only his face, which was a mass of wrinkles, betrayed his great age.

The king had two sons, but they were half brothers who looked nothing alike. One was named Gilla, whose mother had been from the fir dearg, the Red Folk tribe: he was small and red-faced with a large bulbous nose and a mass of red hair and freckles. His clothing was of differing shades of red and bronze, and his temper was just as fierce.

And then there was Seamus Ban. His mother had been Niall's second wife, and she had been from the leprechaun tribe, which made Seamus a full-blooded leprechaun. Seamus was tall and thin, with coal-black hair.

When Seamus and Gilla were called, their father was standing in the prow of the boat, his left arm wrapped around the neck of the huge dragon-shaped figurehead, his right hand shading his eyes. He peered through the shifting clouds of fog and dust that had surrounded the ships since they had left the De Danann isle. Seamus stood on his father's right-hand side, while Gilla took up the position on his left.

Without looking at either of them, Niall spoke very softly. "We must find land soon. Our supplies cannot last much longer."

He suddenly turned around and leaned with his back against the figurehead, his arms folded across his barrel chest. He looked at each of the boys in turn. When he spoke again, his voice was low and serious. "You know that there will come a day when I will leave this world and go on the last great journey that every living creature makes. I am no longer young, and that day draws ever nearer. I must choose a successor—I must decide which one of you will be King of the Small Folk, king of the leprechauns."

"I am the firstborn," Gilla said immediately.

Niall nodded. "You are, but you are not pure-blooded leprechaun. And while Seamus Ban is, he is the second born. If the truth is to be told, then neither of you can claim kingship. However, I have reached a decision . . ."

"What sort of decision?" Seamus asked quietly. He was aware that his half brother was glowering at him, his face becoming redder and redder. Gilla was two years older than Seamus, and there was little brotherly love between them.

"I have decided to set both of you a task. Whichever one of you completes that task will be the new king of the leprechauns."

"That sounds easy enough," Gilla said. "I'm stronger and faster than Seamus Ban, so it should be no problem."

Niall smiled. "Ah, but I'm not going to give you a simple test of strength or speed; this task will require skill and cunning." He stepped away from the figurehead and took two steps before he stopped and looked back at the half brothers. "Whoever finds land—new land, fresh green land—for our people will be the next king of the leprechauns."

And then he turned and walked away, leaving the half brothers looking at each other in amazement. Finally, Gilla left, too. "Don't bother looking," he told Seamus roughly. "I will find the land. I will be king of the leprechauns."

In the days that followed, both Gilla and Seamus poured over the few De Danann books and charts that had been brought along, looking for anything—a clue, a hint, a suggestion—that might give them some indication of where new land might lie.

They found nothing.

Finally, Seamus decided that there was nothing more he could do—the charts showed nothing, the sailors knew nothing. Maybe there was no land, he thought. Maybe they were doomed to sail on until they fell off the edge of the world.

Seamus went and stood beside the figurehead, staring out at the great banks of fog, listening to the waves slapping against the sides of the craft, and dreaming of land.

And that was when he spotted the bird.

For a single moment, Seamus wondered if it was a figment of his imagination and the fog. It was the first creature he had seen since the Small Folk had left the De Danann isle. And where there were birds, there was land . . .

Seamus's excited shouts brought the whole crew running, but by the time they had gathered around, the bird had vanished back into the fog.

He pointed into the shifting wall of gray. "There was a bird, a seabird, with a black head and black-tipped wings," he shouted excitedly. "It must have been heading toward land . . ."

"Well, there's no bird there now," Gilla said, his eyes small and black in his red face.

"There was!" Seamus insisted.

"I don't believe you," his half brother said with a sneer.

Niall raised both hands. "Tell us," he said quietly, "which way did it go?"

Seamus pointed with his right hand.

"And when you saw it, was it moving in a straight line?"

The taller boy nodded.

Niall looked at the navigator. "Follow that course."

"But, sire," the leprechaun navigator protested, "we could be turning in a circle . . ."

"Follow it!" Niall commanded.

The metal craft swung ponderously in the gray ocean and followed the direction Seamus had given. It held to that course for the rest of the morning. At first most of the leprechaun crew lined the rails, anxiously peering through the shifting banks of fog, but there were no further sightings of the bird.

And there was no sign of land.

Seamus's stomach felt as though it had been filled with pebbles of uncertainty.

Around noon, when even the king was beginning to look doubtful, and Gilla's smile was becoming broader and broader, Seamus caught a flicker of movement out of the corner of his eye. Shading his eyes with his hand, the boy squinted hard . . .

A large black-headed seabird had appeared out of the fog, its broad wings beating strongly.

Moments later the fog cleared and a small green island rose up out of the sea before them. The Small Folk started cheering, and their joyous cries echoed across the waters.

Seamus was a hero. He would be the next king of the leprechauns . . . for he had discovered the island that would one day become the land of Erin.

The
Master Builder

Many stories are told about the Goban Saor, the famous wandering builder and stonemason. He was a strange mysterious creature—not fully human, but not part of the Otherworld either. Usually, he would appear in some small town with his son, build a church, a tower, or even a bridge, and then disappear in the night before he could be paid. He once said that a person's thanks and the joy of building was payment enough.

The Goban Saor could not be hired, and though many people offered him huge sums to work for them, money was no object— he chose what he wanted to work on.

Not everyone who approached him was human. The Devil once tried to trick him into building a bridge out of Hell, and on one occasion, the Queen of the Otherworld asked him to build a palace in her fort deep beneath the ground . . .

Early one morning in the middle of summer, the Goban Saor and his son, Cathal, were just finishing their breakfast when there was a gentle knock on the door.

The Goban Saor glanced out through the half-open window. The sun was still below the horizon and the night stars still sparkled in the purple sky. "It's early," he murmured, glancing across at his wife, Moire. "I wonder who that can be?"

"Trouble," said his wife, who had a touch of fairy-blood in her. She was able to see the fairy-folk and sometimes even tell the future.

"Well, if it's trouble, don't answer it," Cathal said, looking at his parents. He lifted the carved wooden mug that his father had made for him and swallowed down the last of his milk.

There was another knock on the door. It was harder this time.

"Don't answer it," Moire said, frowning deeply. "It means trouble, I'm sure of it."

"But there might be something wrong," the Goban Saor protested, looking from his wife to the door.

The third time the knock was so loud that the door rattled in its frame.

"Well, if I don't answer them, we'll be needing a new

door," the Goban Saor said, pushing his chair away from the table and stamping over to the door. He was a short, bald, broad man, with a wide face, and his eyes were the color of the sea on a summer's day. His hands were huge; it was commonly believed that he was the strongest man in Erin.

"Who's there?" he called, leaning against the door and pressing his pointed ear against the polished wood.

There was no reply.

Cathal got up from the table and joined his father by the door. He looked much like the Goban Saor, except that he was a little taller, his hair was a deep brown and his eyes, like his mother's, were green. Although he was only thirteen years old, he was already stronger than most fully grown men. He lifted the heavy stone-mason's hammer from the toolbox by the door.

"Who's there?" the Goban Saor called again. Then he quickly flung open the door and dashed outside. Cathal ran after him into the misty morning.

There was no one outside.

The Goban Saor looked troubled. He threw back his head and breathed in the chilly morning air. He could smell the damp dew, the rich earth, and the distant salt of the sea. He could even smell the odor of the nearby rabbits in their burrow and the mustiness of wet feathers and straw from a sparrow's nest in the trees above. But he could smell no other odors, no smell of men or beasts. Kneeling on the ground, he examined the doorstep for any sign of footprints, but there were none.

Cathal tapped his father on the shoulder and silently pointed to the door-knocker, which was battered and twisted out of shape.

The Goban Saor ran his fingers across the twisted metal.

"Who could have done this?" Cathal whispered, looking at the door-knocker in amazement. His father had made the knocker from a piece of curiously shaped metallic stone Cathal had seen falling from the sky. It had taken all of the Goban Saor's great strength and skill to shape the strong stone. "It would have taken incredible force to do this sort of damage," Cathal said.

"I don't like it," the Goban Saor said, looking back over his broad shoulder at the neat little garden. "It looks like fairy-work to me."

Cathal followed his father back inside the house. And then they both stopped in astonishment, for sitting calmly at the table were two strangers.

They were tall, thin men, with pale faces and eyes the color of wet grass. They were wearing long green cloaks of shimmering metallic material, and two silver helmets rested on the table beside them.

Moire looked up as her husband and son came in. Her face was expressionless as she nodded at the two strangers. "*Sidhe*-folk," she said calmly. "I told you it would be trouble."

The two strangers stood up, their cloaks opening a little to reveal that they were wearing beautiful silver armor over chain mail. Each one also wore a jeweled sword and a knife on his belt. They both bowed slightly. They were so alike that they might have been twins.

"You are the Goban Saor?" one of them asked.

The stonemason nodded. "I am the Goban Saor— but before you start, I'm not working today, and I certainly don't like to see strangers come uninvited into my home."

"And you damaged the knocker," Cathal added.

The knight standing before him bowed slightly. "I am sorry. I sometimes forget that the *Sidhe*-folk are far stronger than humans. We will see that it is repaired."

"I do my own work," the Goban Saor said quickly. "Now what do you want?"

"We have a task for you," one of the *Sidhe*-knights said.

The second knight stepped forward. He smiled, showing shining pointed white teeth. "I am Net," he said, "Chief advisor to Maeve, Queen of the *Sidhe*. This is my son Ronan. I have been sent here by the queen because she wishes you to build her a palace." He paused, then said, "Think about that: the opportunity to design and build a palace for the Queen of the Otherworld."

"What sort of palace?" the Goban Saor asked. Despite his best efforts, he was curious about their request.

"The design is up to you. All our queen demands is that it will be the most beautiful palace either in your world or in ours. You will have all the building materials you need. We can make gold or silver, diamonds or emeralds or, indeed, any sort of precious metal or stone for you to use. But the palace must be magnificent."

"Everything my father builds is magnificent," Cathal said quickly.

"That is true," the Goban Saor said with a smile.

"Well, can you do it?" Ronan, the younger *Sidhe*, asked, but his father shook his head slightly.

"You must not ask the Goban Saor that," he said. "Of course he can do it—*only* he can do it."

The Goban Saor nodded. "I could . . . if I wanted to."

"You would be well rewarded," Ronan began, but Net silenced him with a quick, angry look.

"This is the Goban Saor—he cannot be bought." Net looked at the stonemason and smiled slightly, showing his teeth again. "But I think the Goban Saor will do it, if only for the challenge."

The Goban Saor considered, running his huge hands across his bald head. He *would* like to create the fairy-palace; it would be the most exciting building he had ever made. And the ability to work with any sort of stone or metal would be like a dream come true.

He looked around at his son and raised his eyebrows slightly. "Well, what do you think?" he asked softly.

"It would be nice to build a fairy-palace," Cathal said, "but can you trust these two, or their queen?"

The Goban Saor then looked over at his wife. "What do you think?" he asked.

Moire smiled at her husband. She already knew that he had made up his mind. She wiped her hands in her apron. "I think you should be very careful," was all she would say.

The Goban Saor turned back to the two fairy-folk. "I'll do it," he said.

Net bowed again. "I knew you would," he said. "Now, when the job is finished, you will receive as your payment a house full of gold . . ."

The Goban Saor said nothing.

"Two houses full of gold?" Net said.

The Goban Saor shrugged and stuck his hands in his pockets.

"Two houses full of gold and one house full of jewels, then," the *Sidhe*-knight said, getting exasperated.

The Goban Saor looked up. "I don't want fairy-gold," he said suddenly. "A friend of mine found some fairy-gold, which turned to dust when the *Sidhe* grew angry with him. No, I want a field full of cows, another of sheep, a prize bull, a ram, and some pigs and hens. *And*," he added, "I want them to be real creatures, not fairy-beasts."

Net frowned. "I don't understand," he said softly. "We are offering you riches beyond your wildest dreams and you ask for farm animals?"

"What would I do with all that wealth?" the Goban Saor asked. "No, give me the animals—I'll be satisfied with them. You can tell me tomorrow morning before we go if you will give me what I want."

"But you must leave now," Ronan said quickly.

The Goban Saor smiled and shook his head.

"He already told you," Cathal said with a grin. "My father isn't working today."

The following morning, the sky hadn't even begun to pale in the east by the time the Goban Saor and Cathal had finished breakfast. They were gathering up their tools when there was a knock on the door, a gloved fist pounding on the wood.

"It's open," the Goban Saor called out, turning to face the door.

The door opened and Net stepped in. He was dressed as he had been the previous day, but now his long dark-green cloak was speckled with tiny drops of water that sparkled like silver beads on the doth. Wisps of chill gray fog drifted in through the open door.

"It is time," the *Sidhe*-knight said softly, bowing to the Goban Saor.

"We'll be with you shortly," the Goban Saor said.

He turned back to his wife. "Now, remember what I told you," he said mysteriously, and then he kissed her on the cheek, gathered up his tools, and walked out into the cold, damp morning.

Cathal kissed his mother. "We'll be home soon," he whispered, and then ran out after his father.

There were a dozen fairy-folk waiting outside in the garden. They were sitting silently on their strange fairy-steeds, tall, thin animals, with flat, catlike eyes. The *Sidhe* wore dark cloaks, with metal helmets on their heads, and they were all carrying tall metal spears. Cathal stepped closer to his father; with the fog swirling and twisting about them, they looked sinister and frightening.

But the Goban Saor wasn't afraid of them. He squeezed Cathal's shoulder gently and turned to Net. "Where's my horse? It'd better not be one of these underfed nags," he added with a laugh.

The *Sidhe*-lord smiled and said something in the fairy-folk's own language. Then Ronan came out of the mist leading a red bull that was taller than he was. It was a huge, broad creature, with fantastically curling horns, but its eyes, like those of the horses, were like a cat's.

"This is Borua, the Red Bull, and it's the only creature we could find that can carry your weight."

"What about me?" Cathal asked.

"You can ride one of our own horses," Ronan said. "But your father is so heavy he would have crushed them."

The Goban Saor shook his head in amazement and laughed. "Come on, then," he said to his son. "Let's get going."

His father held the reins while Cathal mounted one of the fairy-steeds. Even though he was still only a boy, the beast groaned beneath his weight.

Then the Goban Saor climbed up onto the broad back of the red bull. Borua turned its heavy head and stared at the man on its back, steam snorting from its nostrils. The Goban Saor stared back at it, almost as if he were daring it to do something, and finally the beast looked away. Net climbed up onto his own horse, bowed to Moire—who was standing in the doorway, watching them—and then he turned away. He had taken perhaps ten steps when he disappeared into the twisting, shifting morning mist. Without a word, the rest of the fairy-folk followed silently in a line behind him. When the last horse, with Cathal on its back, trotted into the mist and vanished from sight, the bull took a few steps forward after it. The Goban Saor turned and waved at his wife, until he too was swallowed up by the gray dampness.

Moire waited until even the sounds of the riders had disappeared before she turned back and closed the door gently behind her. She wondered when she would see her husband and son again. She also wondered *if* she would ever see her husband and son again.

The Goban Saor glanced over at his son riding alongside him. Cathal was looking up into the sky, where the sun was now just a pale orange glow. The boy leaned across his fairy-horse to whisper urgently to his father. "What's happening? Where are we? And why doesn't this fog lift?" Cathal's hair was plastered to his head with the damp fog, and he was chilled right through to the bone.

"The fairy-folk are creatures of twilight; they cannot stand the sunlight," his father said. "They have lived so long underground now, that the sun burns their pale skin and hurts their eyes. Their magicians have created this mist to protect them until we reach their fort and go beneath the earth."

"Have we much farther to go?" Cathal wondered.

The Goban Saor shook his head. "I don't think so. It would take a great power to keep this magical mist about us for a long time. If we had a long way to go, they would have come for us during the night. No"—he shook his head—"I think we're going to that fairy-fort just up along the coast, not far from the Cliffs of Moher."

He had hardly finished talking when Net and Ronan

appeared out of the mist. They were both smiling. "We have arrived," Net said. They rode forward a few more paces, and the fog thinned out. When the air cleared, they found that they were facing a low grassy mound—the fairy-fort.

Net dismounted and walked to the edge of the mound, just where the ground began to rise. He stamped down hard on the earth and said something in the fairy-language, which sounded almost—but not quite—like Old Irish.

Slowly, a huge doorway appeared in the grassy mound. The doors were tall and golden, divided into four panels set into the metal. Each panel was deeply etched with an ancient Celtic design.

The Goban Saor looked at the doors carefully, and then he nodded. "Good workmanship, that."

The doors opened very slowly. Cathal almost expected them to creak, but they were silent.

Behind the doors, there was nothing but darkness.

Net took a few steps forward, until he was almost at the opening. He raised both hands high and said something in the fairy-language. Immediately a deep blue-green glow lit up the tunnel. The fairy-lord lowered his hands. "This is the way to the Otherworld," he said, stepping through. The fairy-host followed him silently.

The Goban Saor and Cathal each took a deep breath and then followed the *Sidhe* into the opening. Once they were inside the mound, Net turned back and clapped his hands. For a moment, nothing happened. And then the two massive doors swung silently closed.

Now there was no turning back.

The Goban Saor and Cathal followed the host down the long, long corridor for what seemed like hours. Soon the rock walls of the fort changed from rough stone into polished marble. Carved into the marble were elaborate scenes from the *Sidhe*'s history. As they rode past, Cathal looked in wonder and listened as his father told him the stories that were carved into the walls.

When they neared the end of the tunnel, the fairy-host suddenly stopped. Cathal, who had been looking at the walls, turned around and found that they had reached a second set of doors. Unlike the first set, these were plain and had been carved from warm yellow metal. He looked over at his father. "Is that what I think it is?" he asked, nodding toward the doors.

The Goban Saor nodded. "It's gold, all right."

Net placed both hands on the right-hand door, and his son placed his on the left-hand side. They pushed together—and the doors swung open. The fairy-host quickly trotted their horses inside, and for the first time that day, they began to chat and laugh together, pulling off their silver helmets, running their long-fingered hands through fine pale hair. Soon, only Net, Ronan, the Goban Saor, and Cathal remained outside.

"This is the Land of Fairy," Net said proudly. "You are honored—very few humans have ever passed beyond these gates."

"And even fewer have ever come back," the Goban Saor said with a smile.

Net's smile faded. "Of course, you will be allowed to leave—once your task is finished."

"Of course we will," the mason said, looking at his son. "Well, shall we go in?" He urged Borua forward.

Net and Ronan stood aside and allowed the mason and his son to enter the Land of Fairy. Once they had passed through the golden doors, the *Sidhe*-lords pushed them closed behind them, but the Goban Saor and his son didn't notice. They both sat on their strange mounts with their mouths open in amazement.

There was a sky above their heads! A blue sky with clouds and birds flying slowly across it. In the distance they could see the shimmering line of the sea, and off to one side were mountains, some of them topped with snow. There were even houses and cottages close by, and in the distance they could see the jumbled shape of a town.

Cathal turned to the fairy-lord. "But I thought we were inside a cave," he said.

Ronan smiled. "You are."

"But the sky," Cathal protested, "the sea. What about all this?" He swung his arm around.

"Magic," the fairy-lord said simply. "You must remember that we are the greatest magicians and sorcerers in the world."

"If you're so good at magic," the Goban Saor asked, "why do you need me to make you a palace? Why don't you just conjure one up out of the ground?"

Ronan looked uncomfortable. He looked first at his father, and then he shrugged. "You had better ask the queen that," he said finally.

"I will," the Goban Saor promised.

They rode slowly across the fairy-landscape. Net led the way on his silver horse, with Cathal behind him, then the Goban Saor on the huge bull with the curling horns, followed by Ronan on his fairy-horse. They passed fields in which the fairy-folk would stop and stare blankly at the two human riders in amazement, watching them as if they were some strange alien creatures. The Goban Saor, who had seen the *Sidhe*-folk before, ignored them, but Cathal looked at them in astonishment. The people of the *Sidhe* were mostly tall and thin, with long, narrow faces and pointed ears. But there were others who were short and stout, with a reddish color to their skin. They had bushy hair, and all the men had beards. There were others who had brown skin and sharp eyes, and wore green cloth. And once, when they were passing a river, Cathal saw a bald head appear from beneath the water; the figure looked at them curiously with its cold, fishlike eyes for a few moments, before disappearing without a ripple.

Cathal saw strange animals that he had never seen before. There were huge, vivid red butterflies, each one as big as a plate, spread out on some rocks by the side of the road, warming themselves. Beside them, tiny birds, no bigger than his little finger, dipped and rose among the rocks, picking insects from between the stones.

There were fairy-horses everywhere, and he saw more of the fairy-bulls, similar to the one his father was riding, although none were quite so big. He also saw sheep whose fleece was pure gold, and others whose coats seemed to be made of shining, twisted strands of glass.

At last they reached the town.

Most of the houses were long and low like the fairy-mounds; they had no windows, no chimney, and only one door. The lower half of each house was covered with thousands of tiny polished stones, while the upper half and the roof were encased with gold, silver, or bronze.

The main street was paved with polished black marble, while the smaller side streets were surfaced with white stone. It was a very lovely but very strange town, Cathal thought.

"Does this town of yours have a name?" the Goban Saor asked.

Net looked back and shook his head. "There is no need. It is the only town here."

The *Sidhe*-lord led them through the town and down toward a wide stretch of water. He stopped and pointed toward the lake. "The queen would like her palace built there."

"On the banks of the lake?" the Goban Saor asked.

The fairy-lord shook his head. "No, you will drain the lake and build it in the hollow that will remain."

"That's impossible!" Cathal said, but his father held up his hand.

"It's not impossible," he said, "just very, very difficult." He turned back to Net. "I would like to meet the queen."

The fairy-lord shook his head again. "I do not think . . ." he began, but then he stopped and suddenly bowed to someone behind the stonemason and his son.

The Goban Saor and Cathal turned around and discovered a very tall, very beautiful woman standing behind them. She was one of the *Sidhe*, but she was not as thin as the rest of the fairy-folk, nor was her face as pointed or sharp. She had a mane of flaming red hair that hung down to the back of her knees, and she wore a dress of red cloth trimmed with green. Around her head was a thin golden band, and there were golden bracelets on her wrists.

"I am Maeve," she said simply. Her voice was soft

and gentle, as if she were whispering. "Queen of the *Sidhe.*"

The mason and his son bowed deeply.

"I have been waiting to meet the famous Goban Saor," she continued. "I have heard a lot about you. It is said that you are the best builder in the human world."

"That is true," the Goban Saor said proudly. "I am the best builder in the human world—and you'll find none better in this world either."

The queen smiled. "I know; I've looked," she said. "Are you up for this task?"

The Goban Saor folded his arms across his massive chest and rocked back and forth on his heels. "There is the slight matter of the water," he said, nodding toward the lake.

The queen raised a hand and a small woman hurried up. She looked no bigger than a ten-year-old girl, except that she had two horns growing out of her head. The queen pointed toward the lake. "Take away the water," she said.

The small woman trotted out to the water's edge and raised both hands high. She then tilted her head back and began to chant aloud in a strange high-pitched language. The air went cold, and there was a sharp, bitter smell.

The Goban Saor and his son watched in silence as a small white cloud began to twist and curl around. As it did, it began to darken in color. The small woman stopped and clapped her hands together three times. And then the water of the lake poured upward into the cloud.

Within moments, there was only a deep round hole left in the ground. The cloud, which was now dark and heavy-looking, began to drift away, but the small woman stopped it with a word, and then looked at the queen.

"Where?" was all she said, in a strange, thick accent.

"To the sea," the queen said.

The small woman turned and pointed toward the distant blue line of the sea. "*Imigh!* Go!" she said. The cloud obediently drifted away toward the sea.

The stonemason turned to the queen. "You have great magical powers," the Goban Saor said. "I have just seen your sorceress do something I would have thought impossible—even for one of the Tuatha De Danann. Now tell me, if you have so much power, why can you not use your own magic to create a palace?"

The queen didn't answer immediately. She slowly looked around at the empty lake, the town, and the blue sky with its white, fluffy clouds before turning back to the stonemason. "You see all this?" she said. "This is all an illusion."

"An illusion?" Cathal asked. "So there is no sky, no clouds, no grass . . . ?"

The queen shook her head. "The grass, the bushes, the trees, and the animals are real, for they were created by the first of the De Danann folk who came into the Secret Places when their magic was strong. But the sky and clouds are illusion; above our heads there is only the cold gray stone."

"But what about the lake?" Cathal wondered. "That was no illusion, was it?"

Maeve smiled. "No, that was no illusion, and it was no great feat of magic. All that happened then was that the water was shifted from one place to another."

"So you couldn't really build a palace," the Goban Saor said. "All you could make would be an image, a picture."

Queen Maeve nodded.

The Goban Saor walked over to where the lake had been and looked down into the hollow. He rubbed his two large hands together. "Well, when do we start?" he asked.

The queen smiled. "You can start now!"

The Goban Saor and his son worked for over a year on the fairy-palace. The queen gave them everything they wanted, and as many men as they needed. The fairy-palace rose quickly.

The Goban Saor used blocks of bronze for the building, but every now and again he would add a cube of silver, just for effect. He constructed four tall thin towers, also of bronze, topped with pointed roofs of silver, and he put in a lot of tall, narrow windows. The roof was made of solid silver tiles, with touches of bronze tile every now and again. It was indeed the most beautiful palace ever built.

Soon, all that needed to be hung were the doors.

Queen Maeve came to see the Goban Saor.

"When will the work be finished?" she asked.

The huge mason rubbed his hands on his leather apron. "Soon," he said.

"You will tell me the moment the work is finished," she said, turning away.

"Oh, I will," the Goban Saor promised. He stood watching while the queen climbed into her black and silver chariot and rode away. Then he called his son. They walked around the palace, pretending to examine different parts of it.

"What's wrong, Father?" Cathal asked. He knew from his father's expression that something was not quite right.

The Goban Saor shook his head. "I'm not sure," he said, "but I don't think that the queen will let us go when this job is finished."

Cathal nodded slowly but said nothing. This came as no surprise to him; he had always thought that the queen would try to keep them in the Otherworld.

"Do you remember that lovely little bridge we built

for that king of Scotland?" Cathal asked his father. "He was going to kill us so that we would never be able to build another bridge like his . . ."

The Goban Saor laughed aloud. He put his arm around his son's shoulder. "You're a clever lad, Cathal. That's exactly what I'm thinking. This queen will have us killed the moment the job is finished."

"But how are we going to escape?"

The Goban Saor winked. "I've got a plan."

Every day that following week, Net, his son Ronan, or the queen herself would come and see if the palace was finished. But every day, the Goban Saor and Cathal would make up some excuse, saying that they were still short of some bricks, or wood, or nails.

But time was running out, and the *Sidhe* were becoming impatient.

Finally, one Saturday morning when the queen came to see what was happening, the Goban Saor said that the only thing keeping him from completing the palace was a tool he had left back home.

"Tell me what it is, and I'll have one of my men bring it here," Maeve said immediately.

The Goban Saor shook his head. "Oh, I'm afraid that I couldn't do that. This is a very special tool; indeed, it's a magical tool that was given to me by the King of Scotland as payment for a bridge I built him."

Queen Maeve nodded. "I have heard of the King of Scotland's bridge."

"Well, this tool can only be handled by either my son or me, or a member of a royal family. If anyone else touches it, it will melt." He shrugged. "As soon as I have it, we'll be able to hang the doors, and then we'll be finished."

The queen thought for a moment. "Would my son be able to hold this special tool?" she said at last.

"Well, he is a prince of the *Sidhe*. I'm sure that he would," the Goban Saor said.

"Then I'll send him," Maeve said. "What shall he ask for?"

"Tell him to ask my wife for the long straight tool with the curly bit at the end," he said. "She will know what he means."

"I will send him today," Queen Maeve said.

Shortly after the sun had gone down, there was a knock on the door of the Goban Saor's house. Moire put down her knitting and opened the door to find a young red-haired boy, with the sharp features of the fairy-folk, standing on the doorstep.

"You are the Goban Saor's wife?" he asked in a high-pitched voice.

Moire nodded. "I am. Who are you?"

The boy bowed slightly. "I am Ruadh, Prince of

the *Sidhe*, son of Maeve, Queen of the *Sidhe*," he said grandly.

"And what can I do for you, Ruadh, Prince of the *Sidhe*, son of Maeve, Queen of the *Sidhe*?" Moire asked with a smile.

"I have come to fetch a tool so that your husband can finish my mother's palace," he said.

Moire smiled again, and her smile was wider this time. "Ah, I wondered when someone would be coming to look for that tool," she said.

"It's a long straight tool with a curly bit at the end," he said.

Moire nodded. "I know the one." She crossed the room and pulled up the door that led down into the cellar. "It's down here," she said. "But you will have to go down, because I'm afraid of the dark."

Prince Ruadh laughed. "We fairy-folk can see in the dark," he said. He looked down into the cellar. "Where's the tool?" he asked.

"Over in the corner," Moire said.

Ruadh climbed down the wooden steps. "I can't see it," he shouted up—and, at that very moment, the Goban Saor's wife swung the cellar door shut and pulled her chair on top of it.

Moire went to the door and called out to the two guards that stood outside. "If you wish to see your prince alive, bring my husband and son back to me by tomorrow night."

The two *Sidhe* drew their swords and attempted to run into the house, but Moire pulled her hand out of her pocket and held up a small golden cross. The fairy-folk stopped and took a few steps backward, their hands up to their faces, blinded by the light from the simple golden cross. Casting twin dark looks at Moire, they retreated and left for the Otherworld.

The two *Sidhe*-knights returned to their queen and told her what had happened. When she realized that she had been tricked, she went down to the fairy-palace to see the mason and his son.

"You may go now," she said simply.

"What about my payment?" the Goban Saor asked.

"You didn't finish the job," Maeve said, her eyes narrowed, "and you won't be paid until then."

"If I finish the job, do you give me your word that we will be allowed to go free *and* be paid?" he asked.

"I give you my word," the queen said angrily.

The Goban Saor turned around and walked over to the palace. Taking hold of one of the huge golden doors, he lifted it up and held it while his son fixed it into place on its hinges. Then he did the same with the second door. He turned back to the queen. "The job is finished."

"So you didn't need any special tool," she said with a touch of a smile on her thin lips.

The Goban Saor held up his two massive hands. "These are the only tools I need," he said.

✦

So the Goban Saor tricked the fairy-folk and escaped with his life. When he returned home, he allowed Prince Ruadh to return to his own country. The mason, his wife, and his son lived in peace for a long time afterward.

No one knows what happened to the Goban Saor. Some say he and his son still wander the roads of Erin, sometimes stopping and building a small house or cottage, and then disappearing before they can be paid. It is one of the reasons the land of Erin is scattered with so many cottages, forts, and castles, all with a beauty that seems almost like magic.

The Legend
of Rock-a-Bill Island

Rock-a-Bill is an island off the coast of Ireland. It has a curious shape, a large rock with a smaller rock just behind it that looks strangely human. Legend says that it was formed because of a greedy and curious woman . . .

Boann sat back on the low wooden chair and watched her husband strapping on his sword and throwing his heavy woolen cloak over his shoulder.

"Where are you going?" she asked, although she had already guessed.

Her husband, Nectain, picked up a beautifully carved brooch and pinned his cloak across his left shoulder. He was a tall, well-built man, with dark brown hair and matching eyes. He ran his fingers through his hair and sighed. "I've got to go and check on the *Sidhe* Well," he said. He stretched and yawned. It was very early in the morning and the sun would not yet rise for another hour or so, but he had to be at the fairy-well by first light.

"Can I go?" Boann asked.

Nectain looked over at his wife. In the darkness, he could barely make out her shape, although he knew if he could see, her face would be set in an angry frown. Every time he went to check on the well, she asked the same question, and every time he gave the same answer.

"You know I cannot allow you to come," he said. "And you know why—it's too dangerous."

"*Why*, though?" Boann asked. Nectain could imagine her bright blue eyes opening wide.

"Because it's a magical well," Nectain said. "I've told you this a hundred times before."

"I still don't see why I cannot go," Boann said angrily.

"Look," Nectain said softly, "my family have guarded this well for many, many years. My great-great-grandfather was given the task by one of the last Tuatha De Danann to leave Erin. The fairy-lord made him promise that only members of our family would come near the well, and he told him that if anyone else came near the magical waters something terrible would happen."

"Well, I think that's silly," Boann said.

"It might be." Nectain shrugged. "But what happens if the magical waters lose their powers once someone else comes near? What will happen to all those people who need its water to cure them of their diseases and injuries?" He turned and looked out of the window, to where the sky was already beginning to lighten. "I must go." He bent and kissed his wife on the cheek and then, taking his long hunting spear from beside the door, hurried out into the cold, damp morning.

Boann stood by the door, watching him disappear into the swirling morning mist. She knew he would meet his three brothers in the forest and then together the four men would make their way to the magical well. She frowned after him.

Something brushed her leg and she looked down. It was Dabilla, her small dog. She stooped down, picked her up, and held her close to her face. Boann ran her fingers through her pet's short wiry coat, wrinkling her nose at the smell of wet straw. "I wonder what they do at the well?" she said softly to herself.

Dabilla wriggled in her arms, trying to bite her round earrings. Boann gently pushed her head away.

"Unless, of course, there's some magic there that they don't want me to find out about. Maybe it would make me more powerful than they are . . ."

Dabilla whimpered and nuzzled her cold nose against Boann's cheek. The woman squeaked and absently rubbed her cheek against the dog's shoulder. "Next time, I think we'll follow them," she decided. She held Dabilla up in the air with both hands. "What do you think about that, eh?"

The dog barked happily.

Boann didn't have to wait long before Nectain told her he was going to visit the magical well again. Winter was coming on, and many people were falling ill with coughs and colds. They needed the water from the well to cure them. Usually when Nectain and his brothers returned, they each brought with them two large water-skins full of the precious liquid. Only a drop was needed for the local villagers, and then riders would carry the enchanted water to all parts of the country, curing anyone suffering from any sort of illness.

So, two nights later, just before they pulled their thick woolen blankets and furs over their heads, Nectain told his wife that he had to be up early in the morning to go to the well. He paused then, waiting for her to argue with him, but was surprised when she said nothing.

"Are you not going to ask if you can come?" he said.

He heard Boann's hair rustle as she shook her head. "You will only say no."

"But you know why I have to," Nectain said.

"I know," she said.

Nectain settled down and pulled one of the furs up to his chin. "Well, I'm glad we've got that settled."

But he didn't see Boann smile in the darkness.

Nectain dressed quickly and quietly the following morning. Boann seemed to be still asleep, and he didn't want to waken her. But as soon as he had gently closed the door behind him, her large eyes flickered open. She threw back the covers, padded barefoot to the window, and looked out.

It was still dark, but Boann could just make out Nectain hurrying down the path, heading toward the woods. She saw three other shapes moving in the early-morning darkness and knew that her husband had been joined by his brothers.

It took Boann a few minutes to dress and tie her heavy traveling cloak around her shoulders. She strapped a small knife to her belt, just in case she should meet anything in the woods—although most of the animals that hunted by night would be settling down to rest for the day.

Boann pulled the wooden door open a fraction and peered out, but there was no sign of her husband or his brothers. So she slipped out into the dark, damp morning, and set off as quickly as she could in the same direction Nectain had taken.

Something yapped in the small wooden shed built onto the side of the round house, and then pushed its way out through a hole near the ground. Dabilla ran up to Boann, her tail wagging furiously, her short, sharp barks echoing in the morning quiet.

Boann knelt down and picked up the small dog. "Shush, shush now," she said urgently, "they'll hear you." She rubbed behind her pet's ears. "You can come with me," she said, "but only if you promise to be quiet, and stay by my side at all times. Is that understood?" She looked into Dabilla's round, brown eyes.

Dabilla yapped.

"All right, then." Boann put the dog on the ground and then straightened up. "We'd better hurry up if we're going to catch them."

Boann and Dabilla hurried down the thin winding pathway that led into the forest. The woods were not big, but they were very old—the druids said that the trees here were among the oldest in the land of Erin. There was a fairy-mound in the center of the forest beneath which the last of the Tuatha De Danann were supposed to be living. But no one had ever seen the mound. There was probably a magical spell around it, hiding it from sight.

Once she entered the forest, Boann pulled up the hood of her cloak. The trees were heavy with mist that dripped and dropped down onto her head with little sharp stings. Thick banks of white mist rolled slowly through the trees like smoke. It was a little frightening in a way, Boann thought, because it looked as if the trees were moving. Even Dabilla seemed frightened and trotted so close to her ankles that she kept stumbling over the dog as she walked.

And then she heard a sound ahead of her. She stopped, and Dabilla ran right into her legs and tumbled into a heap. Boann bent down and picked up the small dog. "Shhh," she whispered.

She heard the sound again; it was a low, droning noise, with short, sharp little breaks in it. As she listened, she suddenly realized what it was: the sound of voices chanting.

Holding Dabilla tightly in her arms Boann crept toward the sound. It grew louder as she neared it. Soon she began to make out words, and then she recognized her husband's voice:

". . . spirit of the waters, come out now and help us . . ."

His voice sounded funny, strange and strained. Carefully, she parted a clump of bushes and looked out toward the voices.

Boann found that she was staring across a small clearing that was surrounded on three sides by the trees and on the fourth side by the tall heaped earth of the fairy-mound. Through the trees to her left-hand side she could just about make out the gray-blue of the sea. And ahead of her was the fairy-well.

It was a circle made up of quartz stones. The milky-white stones had been polished and smoothed, and there was a strange sticklike writing carved into the stones in gold. There was also a flat circular cover of what looked like solid gold lying on the grass away to one side.

Nectain and his three brothers were standing around the well. They had taken off their cloaks and had left them with their weapons near the base of one of the ancient trees. Boann wondered why they were not even wearing their knives, and then she remembered that the Tuatha De Danann and the fairy-folk could not bear to have iron near them. The four men had their arms raised high in the air, chanting quietly in the old language of the fairy-folk. When they stopped, Nectain bowed his head and spoke to the well.

"Spirit of the Well, we need your healing waters once again. In return we promise to protect and guard you, as we have done these many years . . ."

For a long time nothing happened, and then there was a sharp hissing sound from within the well. Drops of sparkling white water began to spit and snap upward, only to fall back down into the well again. The white quartz began to change color to a light brown, and then a pale pink and finally a deep rich red color.

When the four men saw the change come over the stones, they stepped away and picked up the water-skins they had left close by. Then they waited.

For what seemed like a very long time, nothing else happened. Then slowly, so slowly that Boann was not sure when it had started, the colors within the stones began to dim; just as slowly, they began to brighten again. The water in the well rose upward in a thick solid column that broke just above the tops of the trees and then fountained down in a glittering sparkle of colors. All the water fell back into the well—not a drop hit the ground.

Nectain and his brothers came forward slowly, holding up the open water-skins. They edged the smooth bags under the falling water and carefully filled them. When the skins had puffed up into solid balls, the men closed them and stepped back. When all eight bags were full, the fountain of water began to slip back into the well and the shifting colors in the stones dimmed once more. Soon it had gone.

Nectain stepped up to the snow-white stones and raised his hands high. "Thank you, Spirit of the Well, for this healing, magical water. We thank you on behalf of all the people of Erin. My brothers and I will guard you always." With the help of one of his brothers, Nectain pulled the heavy golden cover back up onto the stones and dropped it into place. And then, without a word, they picked up their full water-skins, gathered up their cloaks and weapons, and headed back along the trail that led toward Nectain's fort.

Boann waited until there was neither sight nor sound of the four men before stepping out from behind the bushes and walking over to the well. She ran her fingers down the smooth stones. They felt cool and silky to her touch.

"I wonder if I could lift the cover," she said to herself. It looked heavy and solid, and it had taken two men to lift it up, but perhaps she might be able to shift it to one side so that she could look down into the magical waters.

Boann put Dabilla on the ground and then, placing both hands against the edge of the golden cover, she pushed.

Nothing happened.

Boann tried again. She dug her heels into the damp grass and heaved with all her might. Slowly, the heavy cover shifted with a grumbling, grating sound. One edge slipped out of the lip it was resting against, and the cover suddenly shifted and tilted. Then it stopped. Boann tried to push it, but it was stuck fast.

Now her husband and his brothers would know with certainty that someone had been at the well. She picked up Dabilla and turned to hurry back. If she reached home before Nectain, no one would know she had been at the well. Still, she wondered just what lay within the well. Boann paused and turned back. Then she looked into the dark opening.

For a few moments she could see nothing—it just looked like an ordinary well. And then she spotted two small, red dots, far down in the water. Her heart gave a thump.

They were eyes.

Boann turned to run then, but she was too late. The water rose up in a solid pillar with a roar like an angry beast. There was a shape in the water—the shape of a tall, thin, wild-haired woman, with catlike eyes. She pointed at Boann. Water shot out from the well and splashed her leg, her arm, and her eye—the water was burning!

Boann screamed in fright and pain. She turned and ran toward the sea, hoping the icy water would cool her burns. Dabilla ran along behind her, yapping and snarling, and when Boann looked over her shoulder to see what her pet was barking at, she found that the Spirit of the Well was chasing her. Boann screamed again and picked up speed.

The Spirit of the Well crashed through the forest in a foaming sheet of water, uprooting trees and bushes, picking up stones and boulders and carrying them along. The Spirit roared, and the sound was like the crash of a wave on a rocky beach.

Boann crunched into the sand. She had just about reached the sea when the Spirit of the Well caught her. It swept up Dabilla first, and then surged forward and grabbed the woman. Boann screamed and Dabilla yapped, but the sound was lost in the roaring of the water. The Spirit of the Well tossed them high into the air and then flung them out across the waves, so that they skipped and bounded like flat stones.

And then the Spirit said something in her own watery language. A change began to come over the woman and the dog. As they moved, their shapes began to shift, becoming rough and jagged. They began to grow. Before they finally sank into the waves, they had both hardened into craggy islands.

There was nothing Nectain or anyone else could do to change his wife back into her human form. None of the magicians or druids were as powerful as the Spirit of the

Well, who wielded the most powerful, oldest magic of all—fairy-magic.

So the larger of the two islands was named after Boann's pet, Dabilla, and in the Irish language it was called Cnoc Dabilla. Over the years it became known simply as Rock-a-Bill, and it can be found off the East coast of Ireland.

The Mermaid's Gift

There is an old story told about three magical cows that came up out of the sea, bringing great riches and wealth to the land of Erin. They were a gift from Manannan, the Lord of the Sea, but first he sent his daughter to tell the humans about these special creatures . . .

It was a bright, hot summer's evening when Eila the mermaid swam up onto the smooth sandy beach on Erin's western shore. The mermaid swept her golden-green hair from her eyes and looked around. The beach was deserted, but there were fishing nets laid out to dry on the sand and lobster pots neatly stacked in small bundles farther down the beach, just beneath the tall, dark cliffs. The mermaid drew up her long, shining tail and decided to wait; there was sure to be someone along soon. While she was waiting, she began to sing, and her beautiful, high, thin voice rang out in the still evening air . . .

Orla heard the singing through her haze of sleep and sat up suddenly, now fully awake. She stood up, walked over to the edge of the cliff, and peered down onto the beach, looking for the singer. She couldn't see anyone, so she walked slowly and carefully down along the cliff tops, looking back every now and again at her father's sheep, which she had spent the day minding. She glanced over at the sun, which was low in the sky, almost touching the water, and guessed the time; another few minutes and her father and brothers would be along to bring in the sheep for the night. Then she could go home.

Suddenly the singing stopped. Orla stopped, too, wondering where the sound had gone—or if it had ever been there in the first place. It had been so beautiful, so wild, so natural—almost like part of the sea itself. Orla was turning away when something caught her attention, and she looked down again; there was something gleaming silver down on the beach.

"Orla!" she heard her father, Cullen Mor, call. "Where are you?"

"Here, here!" She stood up on her toes and waved her arms in the air, and then she saw her father's bright red hair and beard. Behind him, she could make out the red hair of her oldest brother, Conn. Her other brother, Ross, was gathering the sheep.

"Where have you been?" her father demanded, frowning. "I told you to mind the sheep."

"I *was*," Orla protested, "but I heard a sound down on the beach . . ."

"What sort of sound?" her father asked quickly. "Voices? Boats?" He walked past her and peered down at the beach, which was already falling into shadow. There had been some pirate raids farther down along the coast over the past few months and, while they hadn't come this far north yet, he was still worried.

Orla shook her head, her copper-red hair shining orange and gold in the sunset. "No, not that sort of sound. It was like singing."

"Singing?"

Orla nodded. "Singing," she said, her voice full of awe.

"It was probably just the waves rushing through the caves down in the cliffs." Conn snorted.

But Orla shook her head. "No, it was someone singing—and it was down there." She turned around and pointed to where she had seen the spot of silver on the beach. But the light was almost gone now, and she couldn't see anything. "Well," she said, "it *was* there."

"Aye," Cullen Mor said, not sure whether he believed her. Although he loved his daughter dearly, he knew that she sometimes made up stories. He looked back over his shoulder at Ross, his younger son, who was rounding up the sheep. "Well, no harm done, eh? Let's go home."

Just then, the beautiful, high voice began to sing again.

Orla squealed with surprise. "That's it, that's it, that's it!" she cried happily.

"Aye, but what is it?" her father asked, pulling his sword free.

Conn swung his bow off his shoulder and pulled an arrow from his belt. He looked at his father. "What should we do?"

"Get your brother first. Did he bring his bow?" Conn nodded. Their father continued on. "You and I will creep down onto the beach while he stays up here, just in case we're attacked. If it *is* a trap, he can fire down onto them and give us time to escape. Okay?"

"But what could possibly attack you?" Orla asked. "It sounds like a woman's voice. And, oh, it's so beautiful."

Her father looked worried. "Aye, that it is; perhaps just a little too beautiful. Let's hope it's not a banshee, eh?"

"A fairy-woman?" Orla whispered, frightened now. She had often heard about the terrible banshee, a fairy-woman who would come and sing outside someone's house, warning them of death.

Ross came running up with Conn. Although there was nearly two years between the two boys, they looked almost identical. Ross was the same height as his brother, and he had the same bright red hair and green eyes. But he was sweet to Conn's bitter. He grinned widely as he knelt down and fitted an arrow to his bow.

"What's so funny?" Orla asked.

Ross looked at her and winked. "I haven't had this much fun in weeks," he said. "Mysterious voices down on the beach, Father and Conn going down to investigate, swords, spears, and bows and arrows at the ready, and me up here to shoot down anything that attacks them. Why, it's the sort of thing stories are made of."

Orla smiled too. Suddenly, they both heard a voice

drifting up from the beach below. The singing had stopped and a woman spoke.

"You have nothing to fear from me."

Down on the beach, both Conn and his father dived for the ground, taking cover.

"I'm not going to harm you," the voice said. "I am alone, I promise."

"Who are you?" Conn asked, talking loudly, while his father crept around behind the woman.

"My name is Eila," the woman said.

"What are you doing on our beach?"

"*Your* beach?" Eila said. "When did this become your beach?" There was a touch of anger in her voice now.

"Our farm is up yonder, beyond the cliffs. This beach is part of our property."

"This beach—and all the seashores of Erin—are the property of the Lord of the Sea, and the Sea-Folk," she answered.

"And who is this Lord of the Sea?" Conn asked, trying to keep the woman's attention on him. He could see that his father was almost up at the rock where the woman was hiding.

"Manannan is the Lord of the Sea," Eila said proudly. "He is my father." She suddenly screamed as a man darted around the rock with a long spear in his hand. He stopped, shocked to find a woman with a fish tail instead of feet, and shouted in surprise. Eila leaned back against the stone and swept upward with her long tail, knocking the spear from the man's hands and sending him backward with fright. Eila dived for the sea. There was a thin buzzing sound, and something long and hard zipped into the sand by her outstretched arm. Another whizzed into the sand by her tail, and a third cracked against the stone, shattering into two. She stopped, knowing she would not reach the water.

"Stay where you are," a voice called from the distance.

Conn came running up, his bow ready, pointing at the mermaid. He helped his father up. "Are you all right?"

"Aye." Cullen Mor nodded. "She just gave me a scare. I'm all right. You'd better tell your brother and sister to come down."

After his son had crunched off up the beach, Cullen Mor turned back to the mermaid. "I'm sorry for all the . . ." He stopped; he couldn't think of the correct word, so he just shrugged. After all, what do you say to the first mermaid you've ever met just after you've tried to kill her?

Eila smiled. "I'm sorry for frightening you. My name, by the way, is Eila, Princess of the Waves, daughter of Manannan, Lord of the Sea."

"I am Cullen Mor," he said. "That was my son, Conn; the one who was up on the cliff shooting down at you is Ross, and my daughter Orla is there also. She was the first to hear you. But what are you doing here?"

"My father sent me with a message," she said.

"What sort of message?" the man asked.

Eila hesitated. "My father said that I was only to tell it to a lord of the land. It's a message for the king."

Cullen Mor smiled. "I am lord of most of the west coast of Erin. If you have a message you wish to have passed on to the king, I will make sure he gets it. In fact, I'll even send my son Conn to deliver it."

The mermaid smiled and nodded as Conn returned with his brother and sister. "My father has always loved the land of Erin, and he has watched over it in many little ways ever since he made his home beneath the Isle of Mona. Now, to show his great love for this country, he is going to send three of his magical cows ashore."

"Cows?" their father said.

"Magical cows?" Ross asked excitedly.

Eila nodded. "Aye; one cow alone can produce enough milk in a single morning to feed a thousand men. Each cow will give birth to a hundred fine cattle every year, and each of these, in turn, will also give fine milk and produce many calves. These magical cows will never sicken, and will never die."

Their father had become more and more excited as the mermaid told them about the cows. Whoever had these magical cows would be fabulously wealthy.

"And these cows are for the king?" he asked, unable to hide the envy in his voice.

But surprisingly, the mermaid shook her head. "No. No one is allowed to keep these cattle. They must be allowed to roam free at all times—otherwise, who knows what might happen? Let the animals wander where they wish; if they want to stay with any particular herd of cattle, then let them. They are to be left alone. And that is what you must tell the king."

Their father nodded, a bit sullen. "Conn will ride to the court at Tara at first light and give your message to the king in person."

Eila nodded. "Then, in exactly one month's time, the three magical beasts will rise up out of the water at this very spot."

"We will be here," Cullen Mor promised.

"I shall see you in one month's time, then," Eila said, and then she threw herself forward and splashed into the waves. For a few moments her head bobbed on the water, and then, with a wave of her hand, she turned and flipped down into the deep dark sea, and was gone.

The month passed quickly, and soon all the lords and their ladies began making their way westward for the big event. The tall dark cliffs sprouted brightly colored tents like flowers. The king and queen were the last to arrive.

King Cormac rode in a beautiful chariot pulled by two golden-brown horses. Behind him, his queen and her ladies rode in smaller decorated chariots. They were guarded by a hundred of the finest warriors in the land. With the early-morning sun shining on their polished armor and weapons, they looked like bronze statues come to life.

The king swung his chariot around in a tight circle and came to a stop before Cullen Mor and his two sons. "I got your message," he said, nodding to Conn.

Cullen Mor bowed slightly. "I am honored that you decided to come."

The king smiled. "I could hardly refuse, now could I?" he said. The king was a small man, with sandy-colored hair and a thin beard that matched the color of his eyes. "I suppose we should go down onto the beach."

Cullen Mor nodded and led the way down to the beach along the thin, winding path, his sons trailing behind them. As they were crunching their way out toward the waves, Ross pointed out at the sea. "Look!"

In the distance, the pale blue water was bubbling and frothing. Long streamers of white water shot upward, and there was a low hissing, sizzling noise. Suddenly the water shot up in a huge fountain that broke when it touched the sky and then fell down again in two beautiful half circles. A dozen small rainbows immediately formed in the dancing waters and sparkled across the early-morning sky.

The fountain slowly died down, and the water grew still again. Then hundreds of tiny bubbles began to break on the surface of the water with little popping sounds. A larger bubble began to form. It grew bigger and bigger, changing color all the time, from a bright blue to a pale white, until it was a huge milk-white ball. Then it slowly began to roll across the waves toward the beach.

The king, Cullen Mor, and his sons backed away quickly, moving farther and farther up the beach. The soldiers on the cliff tops tightened their grip on their spears, ready to attack the huge bubble if it came too close to their king.

The huge white bubble continued rolling silently toward the shore, until an extra-large wave came up behind it and pushed it up onto the beach. The bubble bounced up onto the sand and rolled across the stones—and then it burst, with a wet pop and a hiss, splashing everyone on the beach and along the top of the cliffs with warm, salty water. People immediately began rubbing their stinging eyes. When they looked again, they found three large cows standing patiently on the wet sands.

The animals looked like ordinary cows, except that they were a little larger, their heads a little bigger, their legs a little thinner. One was completely white, another completely black, and the third was a dull red color.

Everyone was staring at them in amazement when a

golden-green head popped up out of the water offshore, and a thin brown arm waved in the air. It was Eila.

"This is my father's gift to the people of the land of Erin. They are the Bo-Fionn," she said, pointing to the white cow; "the Bo-Dubh," pointing to the black cow; "and the Bo-Ruadh." She pointed to the red-colored animal. "Remember, they must be allowed to roam free. They must never be taken by any man for his use only." With that warning, the mermaid waved again and then disappeared into the waves with a flip of her tail.

The three cows wandered slowly up the beach and then along the thin pathway that led to the cliffs. When they reached the cliff top, they continued on down the trail heading for the road. One of the king's men stepped into their path to try to stop them, but the animals just kept walking straight on. When he stepped right in front of a cow, it just butted him aside with its large head.

"Let them go," the king ordered. "And don't touch them."

The cows continued walking down the trail, with the king and his followers walking along behind them. Once they reached the road, the cows turned and headed for the crossroads, where they stopped.

Everyone came to a halt a little way away from them.

"What are they doing?" King Cormac asked, just as the three cows split off onto the three different roads, the red cow toward the north, the black cow to the south, and the white cow taking the road that led to the east. Although they didn't seem to be walking any faster than they had before, they were quickly out of sight.

"Follow them! Follow them!" the king shouted to his men. "Take the north and south road. But don't interfere with them no matter what happens."

The men ran to their horses, and soon a dozen men had galloped off along the north and south roads after the cows.

"What about the Bo-Fionn, the white cow?" Cullen Mor asked the king.

The king smiled strangely. "I'll go after her myself. I wouldn't be at all surprised if she's heading for Tara." He paused and added greedily, "It *is* only right that any magical animals should be close to the king."

"Remember what the mermaid said," Ross reminded the king. "The cows must not belong to any man."

"I heard her," the king said angrily. "I do not need you to remind me."

Cullen Mor turned to his sons. "Come, we have work to do." Before the king could say another word, the man and his sons walked away, leaving him standing alone on the cliff top. The king stared after them for a few minutes, and then he turned and looked in the direction the white cow had gone. He smiled that strange smile once more.

* * *

For a few months afterward, all of Erin was talking about the three magical cows. Wherever they stopped, little rivers and wells of fresh water sprang up, and small lakes formed. No matter where they spent the night, even if it was a rocky hillside, the area would suddenly sprout rich green grass. Every morning and evening the cows would be milked, and there was always more milk than could be carried away.

And so the cows rambled on. The Bo-Ruadh, which had gone into the north of the land, gave birth to two fine calves, and then she disappeared. The Bo-Dubh, who had headed off into the south, also had two calves; the last anyone saw of her was the tip of her tail disappearing down beneath the waves as she, too, disappeared.

But the Bo-Fionn was different. She headed off into the east at what looked like a slow and easy pace, but no matter how hard the king and his men tried, they couldn't catch up with her. She was always just a little bit ahead of them; always disappearing over the top of a hill when they caught sight of her, or climbing out of a river on the opposite bank, or reaching the other side of a bridge before them.

But when they finally arrived at the king's palace at Tara, after their long and arduous journey, the white cow was grazing contentedly in the lush green fields at the foot of the palace walls!

The king clapped his hands triumphantly. "I knew she was a gift for me. Why shouldn't the Lord of the Sea give a gift to the greatest king that Erin has ever seen?"

Everyone looked a little surprised at that. Though he was not a very bad king, Cormac wasn't a particularly good one either. He had done no brave deeds, nor won any great battles.

"Leave the cow where she is," the king said to one of his generals. "But have your men build a fence from there to there." He pointed out across the fields.

The king's druid, who had come out to greet them upon their return, began to speak. "Your Majesty, I must warn you . . ." But the king shook his head and raised one hand.

"This animal was meant for me. The Bo-Ruadh and the Bo-Dubh can wander where they will, but the Bo-Fionn belongs to me!"

The druid shook his head. "That is not so—and you do not realize what will happen . . ."

But the king just ignored the old man and rode off. The old druid watched him, shaking his head in sorrow. He feared for the king and his court.

* * *

Nothing happened for three months.

In that time, the Bo-Fionn seemed quite content to wander around the huge field that the king's men had fenced in. The field bloomed, and the grass there was greener and thicker than at any other place around Tara.

And then one morning the Bo-Fionn tried to leave the field. She ambled up to the thick wooden fence and butted it with her head. The whole fence shook and wobbled. The cow hit it again and again, and then one piece of wood cracked loudly. But the noise brought the king's guards running, and they drove the cow away from the broken piece of wood with their spears while carpenters repaired the break. That morning, the king ordered the fence strengthened and thickened, and the carpenters worked for the next three days strengthening the wood in the fence.

Over the next few weeks the Bo-Fionn tried to break out again, but the king placed guards around the fence that drove the animal back. Every time the cow failed to break free, she would throw back her head and moo piteously . . .

Far away, in *Tir Fo Thuinn*—the Land Beneath the Waves—Eila heard the cow's sad lowing, and she hurried to tell her father, the Lord of the Sea.

"They won't let the Bo-Fionn go," she said in her

strange watery language, her long tail flicking to and fro in annoyance.

Manannan sat up on his throne of polished white coral. He was a tall man who looked almost human, except that his skin and hair were a greenish color and his fingers were joined together by a thin web of flesh.

"Why do they mock my gifts?" he demanded in his low rumbling voice. Far, far above, white waves dashed against the shores of the Isle of Mona. "Someone up there is very greedy." He reached out for a huge seashell and touched it with his fingertips. The inside of the shell glowed green-blue; the colors flowed and shifted across its surface. Suddenly, they steadied, and Manannan and Eila found themselves looking at a picture of the Bo-Fionn trapped behind a thick and solid fence, while the mortal king looked on and laughed.

The Lord of the Sea was enraged. And his anger upset the sea. Up above his watery palace, on the surface of the water, a terrible storm lashed against Mona's shores, engulfing the small island. But at last, Manannan thought of a plan, and his mood changed so quickly that the storm above immediately died down and the sea became as calm as a rock pool. The mortal king would learn his lesson . . .

*   *   *

Cormac still showed no sign that he was going to let the Bo-Fionn go. Even his beautiful wife, Tuathla, came to him and begged him to free the magical cow, but he still refused.

"You were not supposed to keep her," she snapped. She was a tiny woman, with long flowing black hair and hard black eyes, and she had a terrible temper. "Let that cow go this minute!"

"I will not," the king shouted.

"Well, if you won't, I will!" Tuathla suddenly turned around and ran out the door. The king could hear her heels clicking on the stone floor as she disappeared into the distance.

The king sat on his throne and thought. Tuathla wouldn't let the cow go, would she? She was his wife, and he was the king, and he gave the orders, didn't he? Then the king remembered all the other times Tuathla had laughed at his orders and done what she wanted. Suddenly he was up and running down the corridor after her.

"Tuathla, Tuathla, come back! Don't you dare go near that animal!" The king ran out into the courtyard, but there was no sign of the queen. He turned to a surprised-looking guard. "Where is she? Which way did she go?"

The man could only point toward the fields, and then the king was off, running as fast as he could, shouting

Tuathla's name. The guard hesitated a few moments and then he too took off after the king.

By the time Cormac reached the field, Tuathla was already standing beside the Bo-Fionn, the wide gate to the fence swinging open. The queen was stroking the cow's large head, running her fingers down its silken coat.

"Tuathla, stop it," the king shouted.

"I will not," the queen snapped, and then, grabbing a handful of the cow's fleshy skin, she pulled herself up onto its broad back. Using her knees, she began to urge the animal toward the open gate.

The king, seeing what she was going to do, ran to the gate and began to push it closed. The guard came running up then and helped him. Slowly but surely, the heavy gate swung closed. The king snapped the wooden bar across it and smiled broadly.

"You can come out now," he said. "That animal's not escaping."

But even as he was speaking, the Bo-Fionn was beginning to trot and then to run toward the gate. Tuathla held on tightly with both hands. Just as it reached the fence, it bunched its hind legs and jumped.

The Bo-Fionn soared over the terrified king's head and landed with a solid thump on the road with Tuathla still on its back. It gave a huge bellow and galloped off down the road in a cloud of white dust.

It was never seen again.

The king sent guards all over Erin looking for his queen or any trace of the white cow, but they found nothing. The king himself died shortly afterward, a sorry, lonely man.

No one knows what happened to Tuathla or the white cow, but many years later when Orla, the little girl who had first heard the mermaid singing, was walking along the cliff top with her own daughters, she thought she saw something in the distance. It was a huge white cow leaping and jumping among the waves with a small human woman and a mermaid on its back, laughing together.

The Salmon of Knowledge

Finn was one of the wisest of the old Irish warriors; a tall, proud man, kind and courteous. His bravery was legendary even in his own lifetime. However, he had a strange habit of sucking his thumb when he was deep in thought. No one ever had the courage to ask him why, until one day his son Oisin managed to get some sort of answer from him. Still, all Finn would say was that it was because of the Salmon of Knowledge.

The Salmon of Knowledge was no ordinary fish.

It was the length of a tall man and about as broad, and its scales were the colors of oil on water. It was the oldest fish in all Erin—indeed, in all the world—and the wisest, too. Some people said that it was not really a fish, but one of the *Sidhe*-folk, enchanted into the form of a huge salmon. Others said that it was the first creature that had come into this world, and still others said that it was a water-demon disguised as a fish.

But the Salmon of Knowledge was none of these; it was an ancient magical creature. Hundreds of years ago, when the Tuatha De Danann had first come to the land of Erin, it had once been an ordinary salmon. The fairy-folk had decided to hide all their knowledge and learning in seven hazel trees, to protect it from a demon. These enchanted trees had been protected by a magical well, which held the demon. However, shortly after the Seven Trees of Knowledge had been planted, a young girl called Sinann had crept into the hidden forest and attempted to pick the hazelnuts, which held all the secrets and lore of the De Danann folk. The demon had erupted from its well, catching the girl in its watery paws and throwing her high into the air. Then it tore through the countryside, cutting a wide and deep path across fields and through forests until it eventually reached the broad Western Ocean in the west and south of Erin.

People called the mighty river the Sinann, in memory of the girl who had paid a terrible price for her greed. As time passed, and the country people said the name in different ways, it changed from Sinann to Shannon, and so it remains.

However, just as people forgot about Sinann, so too did they forget about the Seven Trees of Knowledge, which stood around the magical well. As the seasons passed, the hazelnuts on the trees swelled and grew, and eventually they fell off into the river. A long, fat salmon came along and swallowed the nuts.

Immediately, it knew all the ancient magic and hidden lore of the Tuatha De Danann. It became the wisest creature in the world. It became the Salmon of Knowledge.

The legends slowly grew up around the fish, and soon people began to try to catch it, thinking that if they ate the fish they would know everything it did.

But because the salmon knew everything, it knew that people would be after it, and it always managed to avoid their traps.

And then Finn came along.

He was still a young boy then, black-haired, black-eyed, tall and thin, no more than ten years old. He was traveling around Erin, learning different arts and crafts. He was trained in the history and geography of Erin and the lands that lay off her shores; he learned how to run and jump, how to use a sword and spear, a bow and arrow. He also learned how to play *fidchell,* an old Irish board game, like chess.

Among the other arts a young warrior had to learn was poetry. Irish folklore and legends were not written down then, but were passed on in the form of long poems and sagas, and warriors were expected to know the legends of their own land. So Finn went looking for Finegas, a famous hermit-poet who lived by the banks of the river Boyne and was supposed to know every legend and tale in the land.

Finn searched up and down the river, but it wasn't until late in the year, just as the trees were beginning to shed their leaves, that he finally discovered him.

Finn parted the leaves of the bush carefully and looked out across the river, toward a small, man-made hut of branches and bushes. There seemed to be no one around, although the fire in front of the hut was still smoldering, and a pan of water had been put on to boil—so long ago now that most of it had turned to steam.

The boy gently eased the branch back into place, making sure no leaf quivered, remembering his training. Look first, then wait, then look again. It was a guide used by hunters when they were chasing the wild boar or deer. Of course, it could also be used for hunting another human. Finn wasn't hunting the famous poet—he just wanted to make sure that it really was the old man, and that there was no one with him.

Suddenly a bird stopped singing above his head. The boy froze. He seemed to fade into the bush; his short tunic of green and his deeply tanned brown skin blended in perfectly with the branches and leaves. Someone was coming. He parted two leaves and peered out again at the little campsite.

For a few moments, everything was as it had been. And then an old man stepped into the clearing. He was quite small and very thin, and was wearing a long robe that had once been white but was now gray. His face was long with a jutting chin and sharp cheekbones, and there were deep wrinkles on his forehead and down along the side of his nose, as if he frowned a lot, but his eyes were a bright, brilliant blue. He was humming contentedly to himself as he sat down on the riverbank and lifted a simple fishing rod from the ground. The rod was no more than an old branch with a length of string attached.

When he had been fishing for a few moments, he suddenly looked up from the still, blue water—straight toward Finn's hiding place. "You can come out from there," he said quietly, his voice surprisingly rich and strong for such an old man. "I know you're in there."

Finn held his breath but said nothing.

"I know you're there," the old man said again. He paused, and then added, "I am only a poor poet; all I have is what you see. I have no money, no clothes, and no possessions—so I've nothing for you to steal."

"I'm not a thief!" the boy said indignantly, and stepped out from the bush. And then, realizing that the old man had tricked him into revealing himself, he smiled sheepishly.

The old man looked over at the dark-haired, dark-eyed boy and laughed. "You see," he said, "there is a power in words. Words can heal and hurt people—they can also make them angry enough to show themselves."

Finn smiled back. "I'm sorry I was hiding—but you can't be too careful these days. I came here to look for Finegas, the hermit-poet, but I wanted to make sure that he hadn't any guests first, or even worse, that I might have stumbled on the wrong camp altogether. I've been looking for you for a long time now." He paused, and then asked, "You are Finegas?"

The old man bowed slightly. "I am Finegas."

Finn nodded. "I thought so." He stopped, and then said, "Tell me, how did you know I was here?"

Finegas shrugged his bony shoulders. "Every bush is quivering slightly in the breeze this afternoon—every bush, that is, except the one in which you were hiding. I assume you were holding on to the branches?"

Finn nodded. "Are you never afraid living here on your own?"

The hermit-poet shook his head. "As I've said, I have nothing worth stealing, and most people are a little afraid of me, and so they leave me alone. Also, I know a little magic—every poet does—and so I can always frighten them away. And now," he said, fixing Finn with his bright blue eyes, "I've answered all your questions. Would you like to answer one or two of mine?"

Finn bowed. "I am very sorry; I was forgetting my manners. I have come here to ask you to teach me some of your lore and poetry. I have been told that no one knows more than you."

"Well, that's one of my questions," Finegas said, "and I suppose it will do for the moment."

"Does that mean you'll accept me as a student?" Finn asked excitedly.

"I didn't say that," the old man said. He stared into the waters of the small, still stream and then a smile crept up across his face. "You know, I've never had a student before . . . it might be enjoyable to teach you a little of what I know." He looked over at the boy. "You'd better have a good memory," he warned.

"Oh, I have, I have," Finn promised.

"Well, I'll soon make it even better," the old man said. "Now, come around here, and we'll start right away." He pointed off down the riverbank to where the humped back of a stone could be seen in the middle of the river. "There's a bridge of stepping-stones down yonder; you can come across there."

Finn laughed. "But I've just finished learning how to run and jump properly," he said. He bent his knees and jumped straight across the river, landing with a thump beside the old poet.

"Well, at least that proves you are what you say you are," he said. "If you had been telling me a lie, you would have walked down to the stones, instead of jumping across like any other young man learning to be a warrior. Here, sit beside me and take this." He pushed the fishing pole into Finn's hands as soon as he had sat down on the damp grass. The poet then lay back flat on the earth and closed his eyes.

Finn had opened his mouth to say something when the old man spoke. "We might as well start now," he said, and then he immediately launched into an ancient poem:

"From the land to the east came the woman with her slaves and her ships fleeing the destruction of her island."

Finegas suddenly stopped. "Now say that back to me," he said.

Finn coughed. "Ahem; from . . . from the land . . . the land to the west, no, the east, a woman came with her slaves . . ."

"*Stop!*"

The boy looked over his shoulder, but the old poet was still lying back on the earth with his eyes closed. "I'm sorry," he began, "but there's no rhyme to it . . ."

"Not all poetry rhymes," Finegas said wearily. "Now, listen to me; this poem tells about the coming of the princess Caesir Banba to Erin with her warrior-women when this island was tiny. She lived on a small island called Meroe in the great river Nile, but when a great flood threatened to destroy the island she left and sailed west—to here. Her sorceress made this island grow, and later the Partholonian people did the same when they arrived, as did the Tuatha De Danann when they landed. Banba, as you know, was one of the earliest names for Erin, and it was named after the Egyptian princess. Now, I'll start again. *From the land to the east . . .*"

So Finn stayed with the old poet and spent many hours every day sitting by his side, reciting the ancient sagas and tales, repeating them after Finegas. The poet spent most of the day fishing, and even when he retired to his tiny wooden hut beneath the trees for the night, he usually left some fishing lines drifting on the water.

But what Finn found very strange was that Finegas didn't like fish, and always threw back any that he caught. Finn often asked him what he hoped to catch, if not a fish, but the old man would only smile and shake his head.

One day, when all the forest flowers had begun to burst into bloom, and the air was rich and thick with the smell of growing things, Finn, who had been gathering firewood, suddenly heard Finegas shout. The boy grabbed his short spear and came running, thinking that some wild animal had attacked the old man. He moved swiftly and silently through the forest, heading toward the river, but when he burst through some bushes onto the bank with his spear leveled, he found Finegas lying back on the ground, struggling to hold a huge wriggling salmon!

"Quick . . . quick," the old man gasped. "I don't think I can hold him much longer."

Finn lifted his spear to stab the fish, but the old man shouted, "No! You mustn't spill any of his blood. Just hold him."

The boy dropped his spear and grabbed the huge fish by the tail. His hands slipped and slid on its wet scales. The fish managed to shake its tail from his hand, and then it cracked him across the head, back and forth, quicker than the eye could see. Finn staggered back, seeing bright spots of color before his eyes, his ears stinging and bells ringing in his head. But he was angry now.

The huge salmon began to wriggle toward the water. Finn grabbed it around the middle this time and lifted it high over his head in both hands. It was incredibly heavy—far heavier than it should be. The muscles in Finn's neck and arms bulged, and he gritted his teeth with the effort. But he held it up in the air until it had stopped wriggling and its dangerous tail hung limp.

Finegas climbed slowly and painfully to his feet. He peered up at the fish and then prodded it with one bony finger. "Is it dead?" he whispered.

"I hope so," Finn gasped. "I can't hold it much longer." He took a step forward and threw it down on to a thick bed of moss. He almost expected it to begin wriggling again, but it didn't move. Finn eased his aching shoulders and then rubbed his face where the fish had hit him. One of his ears was already beginning to swell up, and there was a bruise around his eye. "What sort of a fish is that?" he asked the poet curiously. "It can't be normal."

A strange, greedy gleam had come into Finegas's eyes. "It's a . . . an old species of salmon," he said cautiously. "This must be one of the last ones left alive."

"What do we do with it?" the boy asked.

"Eat it," Finegas said.

"But you don't like fish," Finn reminded him.

"Ah, yes, well, this . . . this old species of fish is supposed to be delicious. I think I might try some of it." He nodded. "Now, you clean it and then cook it on the spit, and call me when it's ready." He was about to turn away, when he paused and looked sternly at Finn. "But whatever you do, do not touch a morsel from this fish before I eat it—is that understood? I've waited a long time to catch this fish, and I think I deserve first bite."

"I won't touch it," Finn promised.

"See that you don't," Finegas warned. "I'm going to rest for a while."

"I'll call you when it's done," Finn promised.

The boy set about cleaning out the fish and preparing it to cook. He started a fire in the small patch of earth that was surrounded by stones, where they did all their cooking. When the fire was burning well, he set up the spit. It was made from two Y-shaped sticks that were set into the ground at either end of the fire. Another long stick rested across them, which Finn put through the salmon, so that the fish was now suspended just above the flames.

Finn sat cross-legged before the fire, staring at the fish, wondering what was so special about it and why the old man was so insistent that he be the first to eat it. The salmon was certainly bigger than any he had ever seen before, and it was definitely heavier than any he had ever held before. But other than that, it looked like a normal salmon; well, perhaps its flesh was brighter and its eyes sharper, but he could have been imagining that.

The underside of the salmon was now cooked, and he slowly turned the spit. Fat and grease spat and sizzled in the fire, and tiny sparks rose up in lazy circles.

"Is that fish cooked yet?" Finegas called from his hut.

"Not yet, another few minutes," Finn shouted back. He leaned forward to turn the fish again. Grease suddenly spat and splashed onto his thumb. Finn wrinkled his face in pain and then popped his burning thumb into his mouth . . .

And he suddenly knew.

He knew the entire history of the land of Erin; he could name the tribes that had conquered the land, their leaders, where they had come from. He suddenly knew the names of every plant and flower, bird, beast, and insect in the forest. He could tell the names of the stars and how they had come to be called that. He knew. *He knew everything.*

He had just tasted the Salmon of Knowledge.

Of course, Finegas was not pleased with the boy, but there was nothing he could do. Finn had been the first to taste the fish, and now he knew everything—even magic. Suddenly the boy was the most powerful figure in all Erin.

And after that, whenever Finn was troubled or whenever he wondered about something, he would stick his thumb into his mouth and call up the magic of the Salmon of Knowledge. Then he would suddenly know everything he needed to know.

The
Banshee's Curse

Finn was one of the greatest of the old Irish heroes. He was a mighty warrior who had many friends both in this world and in the fairy-land, but his constant companion and most trusted friend was his huge war-hound, Bran.

Bran was a magical beast—stronger, faster, and more intelligent than any normal dog. But there was something strange about him, something almost human . . .

One day, Finn and his fellow warriors, the Knights of the Fianna, had been out hunting a band of thieves who had been stealing from the villages. Around noon, they had stopped on the bank of the river Boyne to eat their lunch and wait for the scouts to bring them news of the gang. A warrior from the north, Ilian, walked over to Finn and sat down beside him, resting his plate on his knee. "I've something to ask you," he said.

Finn, who was dangling his hot feet in the water, looked up. He was a tall, thin young man, with dark brown hair and the beginnings of a beard. But you could tell by his eyes that he was very wise, for they were the eyes of an old, old man. "What would you like to ask me?" he said, though he had a sneaking suspicion what the man wanted.

"I would like permission to marry," Ilian said softly, blushing slightly.

Finn smiled. He had an aunt named Tuirean who was a young woman of astonishing beauty, with long, night-black hair that reached to the back of her knees, a small round face, and huge dark eyes. Many young men fell in love with her and asked for her hand in marriage, but she always turned them down. Finn had seen Ilian with his aunt over the past few weeks, and it seemed like she had fallen in love with him immediately. Ilian was tall and handsome, and his hair, like Tuirean's, was night-black. Finn had guessed that this might happen. "Would I know the lady?" he asked innocently.

"Aye," Ilian said. "It is your own mother's sister, Tuirean."

"My aunt," Finn said.

Ilian nodded. "Your aunt. I love her, you see," he continued, "and she loves me. We wish to be married as soon as possible. And because you are my commander, I thought I should ask you." He paused and added, "What do you say?"

Finn pulled his feet up out of the water and began to dry them on the edge of his cloak. He glanced over at the older man. "What if I should say no?" he asked.

The smile faded from Ilian's face. "Well," he said uncomfortably, "if you were to say no, then I suppose we would just run away and get married anyway. But I hope you won't say no."

Finn stood up, and Ilian scrambled to his feet. He put his hand on Ilian's shoulder, and the young man smiled warmly. "Of course I wouldn't say no, and of course you may marry her—but only on one condition," he added.

"What's that?" Ilian asked.

"If I find that you are not good to my aunt, or that she does not like living in your fort, then you will allow her to return at once."

Ilian smiled. "I will always be good to your aunt. And don't worry, I will send a messenger to my fort today with instructions to prepare it for my wife."

Finn laughed and then shook Ilian's hand in both of his. "I hope you will both be very happy together," he said.

"I know we will be."

Even as they were speaking, the scouts returned. They had come across fresh tracks farther down the river, which meant that the thieves were only an hour or so ahead of the Fianna. Finn hopped into his sandals while Ilian ran off to gather up his belongings and pack them onto the back of his horse. Soon the knights galloped off down along the banks of the river Boyne after the gang. Ilian couldn't resist laughing out loud. If they caught the thieves today, he could be back home by midday tomorrow, and he and Tuirean could begin preparations for their wedding.

The day wore on. Finn and the Fianna always seemed to be just a little behind the thieves, and once they even saw them in the distance just riding over a hill. The knights had galloped after them, but by the time they reached the hill, there was a thin column of smoke rising from behind it, and when they rode over the crest, they found that the thieves had burned the bridge across a deep and rushing river. The knights were then forced to ride five miles upriver to find a spot where they could cross over without the risk of being swept away, and of course, by that time, the gang had disappeared.

They spent that night in a small forest not far from the seashore. Along with the rich damp smell of the forest, there was also the tangy salt smell of the sea. Finn posted guards—the forests were dark and dangerous places, with gangs of bandits and packs of wolves and bears roaming through them. Also, the nights belonged to the Sidhe.

Ilian was one of the guards. He picked a spot a little away from the roaring campfire in a thick clump of bushes, where he would be able to see anyone or anything approaching.

The night wore on, and the fire died down to glowing embers. Flaky gray pieces of wood crumbled every now and again, sending tiny red sparks spiraling up into the night sky. Soon, the only noises were the nightsounds of the forest, the gentle hissing of the sea, and the snoring of the men in the camp.

Ilian was exhausted. It had been a long day, and he had ridden far, and he was eager to return home to tell Tuirean that they could be married. He hadn't really thought that Finn would refuse, but he was pleased that Finn had agreed without an argument. Ilian began to wonder what it would be like to be married . . .

Something white moved through the trees. Ilian caught his breath and stiffened. Slowly, very slowly, he pulled out his sword. He waited, trying to follow the movements of the flickering white shape. He wasn't sure what it was, but he was not going to call the camp awake until he was certain. He remembered shouting the alarm when he was a young man for what turned out to be nothing more than fog weaving through the tree trunks.

The shape came nearer. Ilian was sure now that it was a figure—a human figure—but something stopped him from calling the alarm. The shape seemed to melt into the ground, and then someone spoke from behind him.

"Hello, Ilian."

He spun around, bringing his sword up to defend himself, but it got tangled in the bushes' thorny branches and fell from his hands. The pale woman standing before him laughed merrily.

"Dealba!" he said in astonishment.

The young woman smiled, showing her small, sharp teeth. "So you do remember me," she said softly, her voice as ghostly as the wind.

"Of course I remember you," Ilian said. "How could I ever forget you?" He shivered a little then, because Dealba frightened him. Ilian feared the fairy-folk—and Dealba was a banshee, a fairy-woman.

Ilian had met her a few years ago, when he had been doing coast-guard duty, watching the shores for any signs of pirates or bandits attempting to land on Erin's coasts. They had met one stormy winter's night, when the seas had been pounding in over the beach, sending foam high into the sky, roaring and crashing like a hungry animal. When Ilian had first seen the white woman moving up the beach, he had thought she was a ghost. They had become friends of a sort then; coastguard was a lonely duty, and Dealba was someone to talk to and laugh with. It was not until later that he learned that she was one of the fairy-women—a terrible banshee.

Dealba frowned at him now. "I heard that you have a new woman in your life."

Ilian nodded. "Yes, her name is Tuirean, and we will be married soon."

"And what about me?" Dealba asked.

Ilian shook his head. "What do you mean?"

"I thought *we* would be married one day!" she said. "You told me so yourself."

"But that was before I knew you were one of the *Sidhe*. You know a human and a *Sidhe* can never marry."

"You said that you would marry me."

"I cannot," he said.

Dealba's face grew cold and angry. The air around her grew chilly, and frost formed on the leaves and branches. "You *will* marry me," the fairy-woman warned.

Ilian shivered with the cold. His fingers and toes grew numb, and he saw streaks of white ice forming on his armor and glittering on the metal of his sword, which was still lying on the ground. He bent down to pick it up. When he straightened, he shook his head. "I will not marry you," he said. "I do not love you."

Dealba pointed her hand at Ilian and said something in the language of the *Sidhe*. Immediately, the air grew even colder, and then the leaves on the bushes around the man froze one by one, until they were like glass. The branches hardened and turned silver. Ilian's sword grew so cold that it burned his fingers, and he had to drop it. When it hit the ground, it broke apart. The fairy-woman took a step backward and began to fade into the night.

"Wait," Ilian said. He didn't want the banshee to put a curse on him—he would never be able to get rid of it. He reached for the woman, and his arm brushed against a branch. The leaves immediately shattered with a tiny tinkling sound, like small silver bells. Ilian stepped backward with fright—and accidentally touched another branch. It too shattered into a fine silvery dust, and as the man watched, the whole clump of frozen bushes collapsed around him with the sound of breaking glass.

Finn and the rest of the Fianna came running up, swords and spears ready.

"What happened?" Finn shouted. "What was that noise?"

"A banshee," Ilian said quietly, beginning to grow

warm now that the cold had vanished. He looked over at Finn.

"She has cursed me; what will I do?"

"What sort of curse?" Finn asked.

"I don't know—yet."

The captain looked troubled, and then he shook his head. "There is nothing you can do but wait for the curse to catch up with you. When you know what it is, you might be able to fight it."

Ilian and Tuirean were married a week later. The wedding was a huge, happy affair, with all the knights and nobles and their ladies there. It started at sunrise, when the Arch-Druid married them in the first rays of the morning sun, and then it went on all day, eating, drinking, and dancing. Later on there were contests and games. When night fell, the bards came and sat around the huge fires, telling ancient stories.

After the wedding, Tuirean and her husband headed off to Ilian's palace in the north, where they would have a few days to honeymoon before he had to return to his duties.

However, only two days later, a messenger arrived from Finn, asking Ilian to come back immediately. A huge pirate fleet had been sighted off the coast, and Finn wanted all his best men by his side.

Tuirean stood by the tall wooden gates of the fort

and waved at her husband until he had rounded the bend in the road and was out of sight. She was turning to go back indoors when she heard the sound of hooves. She looked back, thinking that Ilian might be returning for something he had forgotten. But it was not her husband—it was a young man, wearing a messenger's cloak. He pulled his horse to a stop a few feet away from Tuirean and climbed down. He bowed.

"My lady," he said, "has my lord Ilian set off yet?"

Tuirean looked surprised. "He left only a few minutes ago—but surely you passed him just around that bend?"

The young man smiled and shook his head. "I'm sorry, my lady, I saw no one."

Tuirean shook her head in wonder. Even if Ilian had been galloping, surely he wouldn't have reached the distant crossroads so soon? "Do you have a message for my husband?" she asked then.

The messenger nodded. He looked no more than fifteen or sixteen, with a head of snow-white hair and a sharp sort of face. "I have a message for my lord Ilian—and for you too, my lady," he added with a smile.

"For me?"

"Yes, my lady. Finn fears that the pirates may land in some of the smaller bays around here and try to sneak south to attack him. He does not wish you to be caught out here with no one to protect you."

"But the fort is guarded," Tuirean said.

"I think Finn's mother, your sister, has insisted that he bring you south for greater protection," the messenger said.

Tuirean shook her long jet-black hair and stamped her foot in annoyance. "Sometimes my older sister is worse than a mother—always fussing." Tuirean left to pack a small satchel and have her horse saddled.

A little while later, Tuirean and the messenger rode away from the fort and headed south. They reached the crossroads by midday, and then the messenger stopped. He leaned forward and pointed down one of the roads. "That way."

Tuirean hesitated. "I thought it was this way," she said, pointing down another road.

"We could go that way," the messenger said, "but this way is safer. It takes us away from the coast, where the pirates might come ashore."

Tuirean nodded doubtfully, but she still followed the messenger down the side road. Soon they rode into a forest of short, fat, ancient oak trees with broad leaves and moss growing on the trunks. There was a little clearing beyond the trees, and then the road continued into another wooded area, where the trees were growing so closely that their branches grew twisted together above the path and hid the sun and sky from their sight. Tuirean had to squint to see the path; she could barely make out the shape of the messenger ahead of her.

Suddenly there was the sound of thunder overhead, and then it began to rain. Hard, heavy drops patted against the closely grouped leaves, spattering and splashing, but very few actually reached the ground. The messenger raised his hand and stopped, but Tuirean was following so close behind him that her horse bumped into his.

"What's wrong?" she asked.

"Nothing," the messenger said, "but there is a clearing ahead, and if we ride across it we will be soaked."

Tuirean peered over his shoulder. Ahead of them, the trees had been cut away, leaving an almost circular clearing through which the path ran in a straight line. She saw the rain then for the first time. It was falling straight down, drumming and thrumming onto the hard ground. Tuirean looked up into the sky, but all she saw were heavy, full-looking gray clouds.

"How long will it last?" she asked the messenger.

He shrugged. "I don't know; not long, I hope."

But the rain continued to pour down, soaking into the hard earth and turning it to soft muck. Water began to find its way down through the thick umbrella of leaves over their heads, and plinked and dripped onto the two riders, making them shiver and pull up their long riding cloaks.

"I think we should hurry on," Tuirean said, pushing her long, dark hair out of her eyes. "We might be able to catch up with Ilian."

The messenger nodded slowly. "Yes, we might," he said, but he didn't move.

"Well, let's go, then," Tuirean said angrily.

"Stay where you are," he commanded.

Tuirean turned to look at the messenger in amazement. How dare he speak to her in that way! "What did you say?" she demanded loudly.

"You heard me," the messenger said rudely. He urged his horse forward, out into the center of the clearing, and then he turned the animal around. The woman was about to speak again, when she noticed something strange about the messenger. All the colors in his clothes, his skin, his hair—even the color of the horse—were being washed away, running like wet paint.

Tuirean closed her eyes, squeezed them hard, and opened them once more. But the color was still running down the man in long streaks. It had started at his head: dark brown rivulets from his skin mingled with the brown from his eyes and ran down onto the front of his jerkin, and then the browns and greens of the cloth dripped onto his legs. The colors fell onto the horse's back, and soon its brown coat was dripping away into a dark mucky pool around its hooves.

Underneath, the man was white—snow white, ice white, cold white. And he was no longer a man, but a woman.

Tuirean looked at the creature and felt her heart begin to pound with fright—it was a banshee! She tried to turn her horse around, but suddenly all the trees around her turned white with ice and frost. A tree cracked with the sudden weight of ice and sleet and fell across her path, blocking the path. She turned back to the banshee.

"Who are you? What do you want?"

The banshee smiled, showing her sharp white teeth. "I am Dealba," she said, so softly that Tuirean had to strain to hear her, "and I have come for you."

Tuirean grew very frightened then. "What do you mean?"

"You married Ilian," the banshee said.

"Yes." Tuirean nodded. "I married him."

"But he should have married *me*," Dealba suddenly shouted. "He knew me first!"

"But a human cannot marry one of the fairy-folk," the woman said quickly.

"He should have married me!" Dealba insisted. "But since he will not have me—I'm going to make sure he will not have you either!"

Tuirean managed to scream once before the banshee's ice-magic touched her. Dealba raised her hand, and the air around her froze. The rain turned to snow and sleet, and the mud on the ground hardened into ice that cracked loudly. The banshee then pointed her fingers at Tuirean, and a thin sparkling line of white fire darted over and wrapped itself around the woman, spinning and hissing, crackling and popping. It lasted only a few moments—and when it had passed, Tuirean had disappeared. In her place was a huge coal-black wolfhound. It glared at the banshee for a few moments and then growled deep in its throat.

Dealba laughed. "If Ilian will not have me," she said to herself, "then I will not allow him to have you."

When Ilian reached Finn's fort, he found that there were no pirates off Erin's coasts, and that Finn had not sent any messenger north for him. When he looked for the messenger who had brought him the message, he could not be found. Ilian grew frightened then, and thundered back to his fort, accompanied by Finn and some of the knights. They knew something was amiss.

When they reached the fort, one of the guards told Ilian that the messenger had come for the Lady Tuirean. And they had not seen her since then.

Ilian, Finn, and the knights of the Fianna searched the surrounding countryside. Messengers were sent across the land looking for Tuirean, but there was no sign of her. And they knew then that she had been taken into the Otherworld.

Nearly a year passed.

It was high summer when Ilian received a message

from Finn. The warrior had heard a strange story about Fergus, one of the western lords. Now, Fergus was well known for his dislike of dogs, because he had once been bitten on the leg when he was a boy. He had not allowed a dog into his fort. But what was curious was that Fergus had been keeping a huge wolfhound for the past few months. And what was even stranger was that Fergus claimed that Finn had sent the dog to him for safekeeping. But Finn insisted that he had sent no dog to this man and wanted Ilian to investigate, so the knight saddled up his horse and set off on the long road to the west.

He had ridden a few miles down the road when something white flitted through the trees and stepped out onto the path. It was Dealba.

"What do you want?" Ilian demanded.

The banshee smiled strangely. "Where are you going?"

Ilian was about to tell her but then stopped. "Why do you want to know?" he asked.

Dealba smiled again. "Perhaps you're heading into the west to visit Fergus, Lord of the Seashore?"

Ilian felt a strange chill run down his back. "How do you know that?" he whispered.

The banshee smiled. "I know many things," she said.

"Do you know where my wife is, then?" he asked.

"I might."

"Where is she?" Ilian thundered. The sound made his horse jump and sent the birds in the trees up into the sky.

"She is with Fergus, Lord of the Seashore," Dealba said.

Ilian knew then. "And is she . . . is everything all right?" he asked.

"She is in good health," Dealba said, then added with a grin, "Fergus has been taking very good care of her."

Ilian suddenly pulled out his sword and pointed it at the fairy woman. "You have changed her into a dog!" he shouted.

Dealba laughed. "I have."

"Change her back," Ilian said, "or else . . ."

"Or else what?" Dealba asked. "I could turn you into a block of ice before you could take even a single step closer. But I will change her back into a human shape for you—for a price."

"And what is the price?" Ilian asked. "I will pay anything to get her back."

"You must come with me into the Otherworld."

Ilian didn't stop to think. "Yes," he said, "I'll do it."

Dealba disappeared in a rush of cold air and reappeared almost immediately with a huge black wolfhound by her side. As soon as the dog saw Ilian, it began to bark furiously and wag its tail back and forth.

"This is your wife," the banshee said, and she

touched the dog with the tips of her fingers. Snowflakes formed on the dog's hair, growing thicker and thicker until the dog was buried beneath a mound of snow— and then it all suddenly fell away. Standing there in her human shape was Tuirean. She cried out with joy and ran over to her husband.

"You've saved me," she said. "I knew you would."

Ilian kissed her gently. "But to save you, I have to go with her." He nodded toward Dealba. "But don't worry. I will come back to you as soon as I can."

"Must you go now?" Tuirean asked in a whisper, tears forming in her huge dark eyes.

"I must," he said, "but I will be back."

Dealba reached out and touched Ilian, and he was immediately frozen within a block of ice. The banshee then touched the ice, and both she and it disappeared in a glitter of silver snowflakes, leaving Tuirean standing alone.

A little more than a week later, Tuirean, who had been expecting a baby before she had been turned into the wolfhound, gave birth to twins. But they were not human twins—they were two lovely wolfhound cubs.

👑

Tuirean gave the pups to Finn to care for.
The greatest magicians and sorcerers in the

land were called in to turn the dogs human, but they couldn't—the fairy-magic was too strong.

Finn named the pups Bran and Sceolan. They were magic hounds: faster, stronger, and more intelligent than any other dog in the land of Erin.

The Sunken Town

Bannow lies on Ireland's south coast in the county of Wexford. It was once the site of a large mining town, but nearly all traces of the town have now gone, buried beneath the ground. All that remains is a ruined church and some gravestones. The spot is known as the site of the Lost City of Bannow, and it is still possible to visit it . . .

Donal propped his bike against the stone wall and waited for his cousins to catch up with him. They weren't used to biking and had been slowly falling behind over the last few hundred yards. He looked back; he could just see them coming up over the hill.

He leaned on the wall and stared out over the sandy hillocks toward the sea. Before him was the small overgrown graveyard, and behind that were the ruins of St. Mary's Church. It was all that was left of what had once been the large town of Bannow.

There was a squeal of brakes behind him. Donal turned as his three cousins climbed off their bikes and flopped to the ground, red-faced and panting.

"*Wow!* You didn't tell us it was so far," Paul, one of the boys, said.

"It's not," Donal said, laughing. He was the oldest of the four, having just turned twelve. He had short coal-black hair and black button eyes that always seemed to be laughing. "It can't be more than six miles."

"Six miles!" Susan exclaimed. "But that means another six miles back." Susan was eleven, two years older than her twin brothers, Paul and Simon. The three cousins came from London but were spending part of their summer vacation in the south of Ireland with their aunt and uncle. She looked up at Donal. "That's twelve miles!" She sighed, shaking her head, her long blond hair catching in the slight breeze.

"It's not far," Donal said, with a smile, "and anyway, it's worth it."

"I hope so," Simon said, pulling off his shoe and examining a blister on his heel. His twin, Paul, came over and showed him a blister on the palm of his hand. They were almost identical except that Simon—who was two minutes older than his brother, as he always told people—had slightly darker hair. Their parents often joked that Paul's hair was the color of fresh butter while Simon's was the color of margarine. But Donal still had trouble telling them apart.

Susan stood up. "Well, what are we here for?" she asked.

Donal pointed down toward the ruins. *"That,"* he said.

"A graveyard and an old church?" Susan almost shouted. "Uh, we have those back home in England."

Donal climbed up onto the wall and hopped down into the field behind it. "Okay, but do you have any buried towns?" he asked.

The twins looked up, suddenly interested. "A buried town! Where?"

"Down here," Donal said. He reached up and helped Susan down into the field, while the twins scrambled up over the stone wall themselves. "Come on, I'll show you where it was." He set off toward the church, with Susan beside him and the twins a little way behind.

They approached the graves, quite close to the ancient church. The twins wandered among the old stones, picking bits of moss and grass off them, trying to make out the dates.

"This is St. Mary's Church," Donal told Susan. He pulled his sweater over his head and tied it around his waist by the sleeves. "Come on, I'll show you the town."

There wasn't much to see. Donal pointed out the long straight lines on the ground that marked the walls of houses and the edges of streets. Here and there, stones broke through the surface of the earth, and there was a short square piece of stone stuck up from under the ground a little way—part of a chimney buried far beneath the surface.

"What happened to the town?" Simon asked after a while.

"Over the years, sand built up against the sides of the houses and began to cover them," Donal said. "When it began to block off the roads, the people in the town decided they had to leave."

"Oh, I thought it had happened in a single night— like Atlantis," Paul said.

"Or Pomp . . . Pompeii," Simon added.

"It took a long time," Donal said. "But in ancient times, it was a very famous town, and the Danes had a mint here."

"A mint?" Simon asked. "What for?"

"For making coins, stupid." His twin laughed.

"The High Street was here," Donal said, pointing to a long grassy rise in the ground, "and over there was Little Street and there was Lady Street." He turned to Susan. "What do you think?"

"I think I'm hungry," she said. She looked at her small gold wristwatch and then looked at the twins. "Go back to the bikes and get the food while Donal and I find someplace to sit."

"I know a good place," her cousin said, and headed off around the side of the church.

The four cousins ate their lunch sitting on a broad, flat stone behind the old ruined church. The sun was directly overhead, making all the children feel warm and sleepy. When they were finished, Donal stood up and stretched. "Do you want to head back now?" he asked.

Susan yawned. "In a few minutes," she said, leaning back on the warm stone and closing her eyes.

Donal nodded. He sat down again, rested his chin on his knees, and stared out over the sparkling waters of the bay, watching the seabirds rising and dipping slowly and then swooping into the water after some unlucky fish. The twins wandered around the church for a little while, but soon they grew tired and came back to the warm stones to lie down.

A little while later, they were all asleep.

Donal awoke first. He sat up slowly and rubbed his neck, which was stiff and sore from where he had fallen asleep. He looked around. Susan was stretched out on the stone beside him, fast asleep with her mouth open, snoring very daintily. A half-eaten apple lay on the ground beside her, where it was being slowly picked over by a long string of ants. The twins had fallen asleep in each other's arms in the soft bracken that grew close to the walls of the ruined church. Donal smiled; they looked even more alike when they were sleeping.

He glanced at his wrist but then remembered that he had left his watch at home. He sat up and twisted his head to look at Susan's tiny gold watch.

Half past four!

Donal was just about to lean over and shake Susan awake when he saw a movement out in the graveyard. A flash of red, and then it was gone. Donal froze, his heart beginning to beat quickly.

He caught the flash of movement out of the corner of his eye again, and he had the impression of red and green and brown . . . and a shape that was almost human.

It was coming closer.

Susan stirred in her sleep and opened her eyes. She raised her hand to shade her face from the sun, but Donal quickly pressed his hand over her mouth. "Don't say a word," he whispered. "Don't even breathe. There's something moving out in the graveyard."

Susan's eyes widened with fright, but she stayed quiet.

The shape continued to approach the church, dodging and weaving through the gravestones, appearing for a moment and then disappearing into the ground. Donal squinted against the sun's glare, trying to make out the shape.

The figure disappeared again . . . and then it hopped up onto the stones, directly in front of the four children!

Donal and Susan screamed, waking the twins, who both began to cry. The figure startled, too. It was a small, red-faced man no bigger than the twins, wearing a bright green coat, a red cap, and a pair of large, silver-buckled black shoes. It waved its arms as it tried to keep its balance on the stones, and then it fell—right at Donal's feet!

Donal gasped. "It's a cluricaun!"

"A what?" Susan whispered, moving as far away from the small man as possible.

Once he got over his fright, the cluricaun got up and dusted himself off. He took off his cap and bowed deeply to the girl. "He means a leprechaun, young lady," he said in a high-pitched, almost musical voice. He bowed deeply to the twins and Donal. "I am Donn Dearg," he said. "Or Red Donn, as my friends call me."

Donal smiled with relief. He knew there was no harm in leprechauns, unless you harmed them or tried to cheat them in some way. "I'm Donal," he said.

The leprechaun nodded. "Yes, I've seen you here before."

"And these are my cousins from London," Donal added.

"In England," Susan said. The twins smiled sheepishly at the leprechaun.

"My lady," the leprechaun said swiftly. "I have relatives in London, England, and also in Glasgow, Scotland," he added with a grin.

"What are you doing here?" Susan asked. "Do you live here?"

The leprechaun suddenly grew very cautious. "I live around here," he said. "A lot of the *Daoine Sidhe* live around here."

"Why?" Donal asked.

"Because it's a very special, very ancient place. There was a fairy-fort here long before the town of Bannow was built." The leprechaun turned his back on the children and looked out over the low mounds and ridges that marked the old town halls. He shook his head slowly. "I can remember when this was a rich, flourishing town, and before that I can remember the rich pasturelands, and before *that* I can remember the old De Danann fort that used to be here. But that was a long time ago."

"Tell us what happened," Susan begged. The twins nodded.

Donn Dearg hesitated for a few moments, and then he sat down on the stones beside them. "I can only stay a few minutes," he said, "but I'll try." The wizened man pulled out a long white pipe and filled it with a fine green tobacco. He whispered a word, touched the end of his finger to the bowl, and immediately began to puff thick clouds of smoke.

"How did you do that?" Simon whispered.

Donn Dearg smiled and winked. "Magic," he said, and began his tale. "The town of Bannow was built on the site of a fairy-fort. Now, while the *Daoine Sidhe* didn't like it, there was little they could do without drawing attention to themselves—and the fairy-folk do not like to draw attention to themselves. So they held a great council and decided that if the Human-Folk did nothing to disturb them, they would leave them in peace.

"And so they did for a while.

"But then the Human-Folk discovered that there was precious metal in the ground around their town, and so they began to dig down into the earth. Well, the *Sidhe* couldn't allow that now, could they?" Donn Dearg asked.

"Why not?" Susan wondered.

"*Why not?* Because they live in the ground, little lady. How would you like some giant digging a great big hole in the roof of your house?"

The twins giggled at the thought of a giant digging a hole in the roof of their house in Chelsea, but Donn Dearg shook his head. "It's not funny, you know."

Donal shushed them. "Go on," he said to the lepre-chaun.

"Well," said Donn Dearg, puffing angrily on his pipe and sending clouds of white smoke up into the clear blue sky. "All the fairy-folk gathered together on the beach down there, and, with the help of some of the Sea-Folk, they worked a piece of the Old Magic."

"What's Old Magic?" Simon asked.

"The most powerful kind in the world," Donn Dearg said. "From that night on, the fairy-folk have been slowly covering the town with sand, burying it deeper and deeper. In a few hundred years there will be nothing left, nothing at all."

"I wonder what it looked like," Susan said quietly, gazing out over the ruins.

Donn Dearg smiled sadly. "It was lovely," he admitted. "In the morning with the sun shining on the white-washed houses, and in the evening with the sun turning the thatch to gold, it was really beautiful."

"I wish I could have seen it," she said.

Donn Dearg peered at her. "Do you really?"

Susan nodded.

He looked at each of the children in turn. "Would you like to know what the town looked like?" The three boys nodded. "All right, then," the leprechaun said. He tapped out his pipe on the ground and put it in his pocket. It was still smoking. "Take hold of each other's hands," he ordered them, and then he took hold of Susan's and Donal's hands. "Now close your eyes."

"What are you going to do?" Donal asked, alarmed. He knew enough about the fairy-folk to know that they sometimes stole children away.

"I'm going to show you Bannow from the very beginning," Donn Dearg said.

Donal squeezed his eyes shut. He felt a cold breeze blow across his skin and ruffle his hair.

"You can open your eyes now," Donn Dearg said. "But keep holding hands—don't let go."

The four children opened their eyes and found that the ruined church and the graveyard had disappeared. Everything had changed. There were trees everywhere—tall, thin trees that stretched up into the heavens, and short, broad, wide-bodied trees that looked very, very old. There were holly bushes growing around most of the trees, and the ground was covered with lush green grass.

There was movement among the trees, and then strange riders on tall, thin horses rode into the small clearing. They were wearing long gray cloaks that shimmered with dew, and beneath their cloaks they wore silver armor and carried swords and spears of silver. They stopped and looked around, and seemed to look right through the children and the leprechaun. More riders arrived, and there were small, dark men with them that looked much like the leprechaun. The taller folk gathered around in a huge circle, joined hands, and bowed their heads.

A blue spark suddenly danced around them, and then it shot out and touched the trees and bushes, turning them to dust. In a few heartbeats, there was a huge clearing in the center of the forest, with nothing but a pile of gray dust to show where the trees had once stood. Even as the children watched, the dust shifted and scattered on the breeze.

More riders arrived, bringing supplies in broad, big-wheeled wagons pulled by oxen. They brought polished stones, black and green marble, smooth slates and shales, and glittering quartz. Soon a palace began to rise in the clearing. The *Sidhe*-folk used their magic to build a tall, strong fort of marble, with a roof of slate and shale, and quartz windows.

Time must have been passing very quickly, because the four children could see the clouds racing across the sky, like a film speeded up, and they saw a wall growing almost magically around the fort. Then more riders came—demon-folk that looked like huge snakes, riding demon horses that looked like dragons. The children saw the blue-white magic of the *Sidhe* battle against the red-black power of the demons. But the blue-white magic was stronger, and the demon-folk were defeated.

Once again time slipped past very quickly, and the cousins saw that there were fewer trees now. They could see the blue of the sea sparkling in the distance.

There were new invaders now: men. They brought with them a most fearsome weapon, iron. And the *Sidhe*-folk had no protection against their iron swords and spears.

So the *Sidhe*-folk left the world of men and went to their Secret Places: the hidden forts beneath the ground, the floating islands in the sea, the Land Beneath the Waves, and the lost valleys.

Years slipped away, and the children saw the fairy-fort begin to crumble. First, a few slates fell from the roof and then one of the windows fell out; soon, the great gate cracked and slipped from one hinge. Grass and weeds soon took over, and then the walls began to crumble and fall to the ground, until eventually— although it must have been many, many years later— the fort was nothing more than a tumbled pile of stones.

And then the fairy-folk came back. The *Sidhe*-folk moved about quickly, shifting some of the stones and digging down deep into the earth, and then the *Sidhe* used their magic on the small hill. The ground heaved up and glowed a bright eerie green, and then a door opened in the grass and the children found that they could see down, far down into the earth. More and more of the *Sidhe*-folk came then and went down into the earth. Then the door disappeared, leaving no trace of it behind.

Time passed quickly again. The cousins saw ships in the harbor, tall square-sailed ships with many oars and with a dragon-shape carved at one end. Vikings. The newcomers built quite close to the fairy-fort, a rough town of wood and stone buildings, surrounded by a tall wooden fence with sharpened spikes. The town grew and grew. Very soon, a building began to grow up beside the children. It was the church. The grave-yard came next and soon spread out all around them. Bannow was now a large prosperous town, with many stone houses, and larger buildings in it.

The men dug mines and began gathering a dull, silver-gray metal from the earth. The metal was brought to a tall building in town, which seemed to be puffing out smoke day and night. It was the mint, Donal thought, where they made silver coins. The mines quickly spread farther and farther out around the town. Soon they ap-proached the site of the ancient fairy-fort. Some men began to dig into the side of the fort.

The cousins saw two of the fairy-folk emerge from an opening in the fort. They looked toward the town, raised their arms, and clapped their hands. They then turned and headed off to the shore.

The forest came alive with rustlings and creaks. The children saw the shadowy figures of small men, tall people, ghostly horses, and others heading toward the beach. From where they were standing, they could see beams of light shoot up into the heavens, darting and spinning, spitting golden sparks and silver streamers down onto the town—but strangely enough, none of the townspeople seemed to notice.

It was a curse, Donal realized. The fairies had put a curse on the town.

Time raced past again, and now the children saw the dust drift in over the town, first creeping up along the walls, sifting through the windows, and then covering the roofs. They saw some of the roofs cracking beneath the weight and crashing to the ground. They saw the crops dry up and die in the sandy soil, and they saw the houses disappear beneath the shifting sand. When they were covered, grass began to sprout on top of them.

The church remained untouched—the fairy-folk's curse must not have had any power against it. But with no people to serve, it soon fell into disuse and then into disrepair. Gradually it crumbled away, leaving only a shell behind.

And then a fog came down—a thick, cold, damp fog that covered everything and made it impossible to see even a hand in front of your face. Abruptly, the fog vanished—and the four children found that they were back where they had started, beside the old ruined church with the sun beating down on their heads.

Donn Dearg let go of Donal's and Susan's hands with a sigh. "That is what happened," he said sadly. "The townspeople were greedy, and their greediness destroyed them."

Susan pressed her hands together and rubbed them hard. She was trembling. "It looked . . . it looked like it was a very lovely town," she said.

Donn Dearg nodded. "Aye, it was." The leprechaun hopped down off the wall and turned back to the four children. "I must go now, but thank you for your time and for patience."

"We should be the ones thanking you!" Donal said. "That was amazing."

"Yes," Susan agreed, "I don't think we'll ever forget it."

Donn Dearg bowed to each of the four children. Then he turned and ran off among the gravestones, disappearing behind the tumbled stones.

When he was gone, Susan turned to Donal. "Was he real? Were we dreaming?"

"If we were, then we were all dreaming the same dream . . ." He looked around for the twins, but they had run off into the gravestones. "Come on," he shouted. "We've a long way to go." He turned and walked back toward the bicycles with Susan.

"You know no one is going to believe us," she said.

"Don't tell anyone, then," he said.

"But I wish we could tell them what we saw," Susan insisted.

"We need proof," Donal said. They climbed up on the bikes and waited for the twins, who were running through the graveyard toward them. They were red-faced and looked as if they were both about to burst.

"What's up with you two?" Donal asked.

"You remember that tall building Donn Dearg showed us?" Simon began.

"The mint!" Paul continued. "Where they made the coins."

Donal looked at Susan and then nodded in confusion.

"Well, we were looking to see if we could find that building," Simon said.

"And we did," Paul finished. "It was over there." He pointed back across the field.

"So?" Donal asked.

The boys opened their hands. They were each holding a small, round, ancient-looking piece of metal.

"What are they?" Susan asked.

Donal picked one up and rubbed some of the grass and dirt off it. Underneath was a silver coin. He turned to Susan. "People will have to believe us now!" he said in triumph.

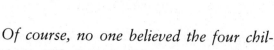

Of course, no one believed the four children. But they did have a hard time explaining away the two silver Viking coins the boys had found at the site of the mint.

The Last Partholonian

The Partholonians came to the land of Erin when the world was young, and Ireland was still a small, rocky island. They used their powerful magic to make the land grow. They pushed back the sea, exposing more and more ground, and soon there was room enough for all, and the land was a rich and very beautiful place. But the fresh green land of Erin also attracted the terrible Fomorians, demons from the icy Northlands. And the Partholonians and the Fomorians fought together many times, until at last the Fomorians were defeated . . .

Tuan wandered across the battlefield on the morning after the last battle. Tuan was the chief bard and storyteller of the Partholonians. When night fell, he would stand up in the great hall and, in his rich strong voice, he would tell his stories so that the people would remember. He would also sing about the great heroes and heroines, about the gods and goddesses and about the strange creatures and monsters that wandered the world in those days.

The sun was low in the sky, casting long shadows across the trampled burnt earth. There were swords and shields, knives and spears, pieces of armor and torn rags of flags everywhere—but there were no bodies. The demons had turned to dust once they were killed, and the Partholonians had taken all their own dead away.

Tuan shivered; it felt strange to be walking where only yesterday they had fought the terrible Cichal One-Foot, the leader of the Fomorians. He shaded his eyes with his hand and looked up at the low hill where the monster had finally been killed—but the only sign that anything had happened there was the long scorch mark on the grass where Cichal's tent had burned down. Tuan shook his head, thinking how terrible it had been and, pulling his cloak up around his ears, walked slowly across the grass toward the hill.

Tuan was an old man now, and he had been a bard for many years. He was very tall, with snow-white hair, and a short, curled beard. His eyes were the color of granite. He was supposed to know the entire history of the world and had once sung nine hundred different songs in one night for a bet.

But the song he was writing now would be his finest tale, he promised himself. It would be called "The Song of the Partholonians," and it would cover their flight from Scythia; their journey along the Middle Sea and out through the Pillars of Hercules, and then their travels up along the rocky coast of the land of the Iberians, across the stormy Bay of Biscay, and finally to the tiny island which they would later call Banba. His story—his song—would finish with the battle with the demons, and the Partholonian victory. And that was why he was now walking through the battlefield. He wanted to see for himself just where the Last Battle had been fought, and what it might have felt like.

"Now, the demons gathered here," Tuan said to himself, looking around. "They had more men—well, demons really—down there, and they were all facing our men who were over there." He pointed with his long-fingered hand across the field to another series of low hills.

"Now," the old man continued, "the demons were

protected by their magical fog . . ." Tuan closed his eyes, and he could almost see the thick red-gray fog rolling about down in the field below him. "And the magical wind that our magicians made would probably have come in from the sea." Tuan turned to look toward the east to where the distant blue glint of the sea could be seen. He imagined the wind gusting in from the sea, rich with the smell of the ocean, whipping away the demons' protecting fog . . . and then the battle had begun.

Yes, Tuan thought as he nodded to himself, it was going to make a great story. He would sing it when the Victory Feast was held. But the feast would not be held until their leader Partholon recovered from the minor wound he had received in the battle. So, there was no real hurry; he had about a week or so.

Tuan crossed the field and walked up the low hill to where the Partholonians had gathered. Already, parts of his great song were beginning to come to him. He decided it would open with Partholon speaking to his men . . .

"Help me."

Tuan stopped suddenly. He felt all the hairs on his head and in his beard begin to tingle, and his heart began to pound. That had not been a man's voice.

"Help me, please."

The voice was harsh and rough, more of a bark than anything else. It sounded almost as if a dog had learned to speak.

"Help me."

Tuan's first thought had been to run; after all, he was a bard, not a warrior. However, now that he had heard the voice speak again, he thought that it sounded very weak. So he carefully climbed up a low hill and looked down over the side.

He was looking at a Fomorian, a demon. He didn't seem to be a very big demon, but he was very, very ugly and more than a little bit frightening. He looked rather like a horse, but a man-shaped horse, with snakelike skin that was all shimmering green scales. His head was horselike, too, except that his ears were too long and he had a black, snakelike tongue. Strangely, the demon also had the brightest blue eyes Tuan had ever seen.

The Fomorian was lying at the bottom of the hill in a hole with one of his long back legs twisted beneath himself. Because the ground was very soft and crumbled away every time he grabbed a handful to pull himself up, the demon was trapped.

The Fomorian looked up at Tuan with his bright blue eyes. "Help me, please," he said, in his rough, barking voice.

"But you're a demon!" Tuan said in surprise. "Why should I help you?"

The demon shook his great head slowly. "I don't know of any reason why you should help me," he said, "except that you might want to help another creature that is in pain."

"If I help you, you'll probably kill me," the bard said.

"I won't eat you," the demon said. "Besides, you're too old; the meat would be too tough and stringy."

Tuan looked insulted that the demon wouldn't even think about eating him.

"But will you help me up, please?" The demon paused and then he said, "If you do, I will give you a great gift."

"What is it?" Tuan asked greedily.

The Fomorian's eyes gleamed craftily. "Help me out first, and then I'll give it to you—it is something that few people in this world will ever have."

"And you promise you won't eat me?"

"I promise."

"Do you swear?" Tuan asked.

"I swear by my dead lord, Cichal One-Foot," the Fomorian said.

"All right, then. You stay there—well, you can't really go anywhere, can you?—and I'll go and get something to pull you out with." Tuan hurried off to look for a length of rope or a long branch. He was halfway across the field when he spotted a long spear sticking into the grass. It was one of the Fomorian weapons; it was almost twice his height and made from a strange black wood. Tuan wrapped both hands around the thick shaft and pulled . . . and pulled . . . and pulled. Finally, the spear came up out of the ground with a squelch.

Tuan dragged it back up the low hill. He leaned over and looked down.

"I've got something," he said, and then he slid the spear down over the edge and into the hole.

The demon grabbed the spear and stuck it deep into the ground, and then he began to pull himself up along the long length of wood. Tuan realized then just how big the Fomorian was—he was *huge*. His front claws dug deep into the edge of the hole, and in one smooth movement, he had pulled himself out. He lay stretched out on the grass, panting loudly. Tuan backed away slowly and carefully, although he knew that if the demon decided to eat him, he had little chance of escaping. The demon's bright blue eyes opened suddenly, and he stared at the man.

"Thank you," he said as quietly as he could, although it still sounded like a shout in his booming voice.

Tuan nodded without saying a word.

"You have saved my life—and now I will save yours," the demon continued. "Now, listen to me. As we speak, a terrible plague is beginning to kill your people. It will start like an ordinary cold—a sore throat, runny nose, cough—but this is much more dangerous. The plague will kill all the Partholonians."

"*Oh!*" Tuan could only whisper, shocked.

"All except you."

"Me?" Tuan whispered.

"You will live; you will be the last Partholonian,"

the demon said. "I am going to give you one of the most valuable gifts I can—an almost eternal life. You, Tuan, are going to live for a long, long time."

"But—" Tuan began.

"There is very little time," the demon said. "Stand straight, close your eyes, put your hands down by your sides, and breathe easily."

Tuan did as he was told. For a long time, nothing seemed to happen. He could hear his heart beating strongly in his chest, and he could feel the breeze on his face ruffling his hair and beard. And then a sudden thought struck him.

There had been no breeze that morning!

Tuan tried to open his eyes, but found that he couldn't. And then he felt his skin tingling, as if pins and needles were dancing up and down his arms and legs. His skin grew cold and then itchy, and then suddenly it felt hot and dry. His hair seemed to be standing on end, and he could actually feel it growing, pushing its way out from his head and chin. He fell forward onto the ground. His arms began to ache, and his legs felt rubbery, as if he had run a long distance. He heard his bones cracking and popping—and then, quite suddenly, it was all over.

But now everything seemed different as he looked around. All the colors seemed to be sharper and brighter—and everything seemed to be somehow smaller. Even the huge demon now looked no bigger than himself. "What have you done to me?" he asked, or tried to, because all that came out was a rough bellowing sound.

The Fomorian smiled, his huge mouth opening wide, showing his sharp yellow teeth. "I have saved your life," he said. "All the men and women on this island will die soon—but you will not, because you are no longer a man."

"What am I?" Tuan shouted, but all he heard was a roar. However, the demon seemed to understand his language.

"I have given you the shape of a wild ox," he said. "The spell will last for three hundred years, and after that you will turn into a white horse for two hundred years; then you will turn into a golden eagle for another three hundred, and you will spend a final hundred years in the shape of a salmon." The demon was about to turn away but stopped. "That is the best that I can do," he said. "If I were stronger or a better magician, I might be able to give you a few hundred more years, but I'm afraid that nine hundred is the best I can do."

"And what happens in nine hundred years' time?" Tuan shouted.

"Then you should turn back into a man," the demon said. "I hope." Then he turned and ran quickly across the field and disappeared over a hill.

Tuan turned away and galloped in the opposite direction. Perhaps one of the magicians of the Partholonians would be able to turn him back into his human shape. He stopped only once, when he reached a very small river. He bent his huge head over the water and stared into it, examining his reflection. Just as the demon had said, he was now a wild ox with thick, pointed horns and smooth creamy-white skin. Only his large gray eyes still looked human.

Tuan galloped on then, but when he reached the Partholonian campsite, there was no one there. It was deserted, although the pots still bubbled on the fire, and it looked as if they had left only a few moments ago. He caught a strange smell on the air. He didn't know what it was, but it was coming from the direction of the beach. He hurried down along the path that led down to the sea, his wide, wet nose wrinkling at the strange smell.

He was still wondering what it was when he reached the beach—and he found the Partholonians. They were all lying dead on the rough stony beach. The plague the demon had been talking about had struck suddenly.

And Tuan realized that he was now the last Partholonian. The huge wild ox raised his head to the sky and bellowed sorrowfully.

Tuan lived for nine hundred years and more. He watched the new invaders claim

the land: the golden Nemedians, the evil Fir
Bolg, the magical Tuatha De Danann, and
the human Milesians. He watched the land
grow green and strong beneath them, and
he watched the people come and go, and all
the time he was learning. And when Tuan
became a man again many hundreds of
years later, he was the wisest man in all the
land of Erin.

Hero

When we think of heroes, we think of brave knights on horseback, wearing armor and carrying spears and swords, doing battle with demons and dragons, evil knights and magicians.

But there are other kinds of heroes; heroes we never hear about . . .

Etan and Ronan ducked down behind the bushes when they heard the sound of the horses approaching.

Ronan carefully parted a few leaves and peered out, down the dry, dusty road that led through the woods toward the lake. For a few moments he saw nothing, and then he spotted a cloud of white dust in the distance, moving through the trees along the road.

"Who is it?" Etan, his sister, whispered.

Ronan shook his head. "I can't see yet; they're still too far away." Ronan was ten, just one year younger than Etan. They both had coal-black hair, large dark eyes, and long faces.

"Can you see anything yet?" Etan demanded.

"No . . ." Ronan began, but then said, "Yes! It's all right, I can see Uncle Niall. He must be returning with the king's men."

The boy and girl stepped out of the bushes and stood by the side of the road, waiting for the warriors to draw closer. If they were lucky, they might be able to get a ride on one of the horses back to their father's fort. Ronan and Etan were the children of Dalbach, Lord of the O'Byrne clan; he owned most of the land in this part of the country.

The riders were closer now, and the children could

see that something was very wrong. For a start, there didn't seem to be half as many of them as had gone out that morning. The few that remained were all battered and bloodied, and their armor was torn and filthy. Many of them had lost their weapons, and none were carrying their tall spears. Some swayed in their saddles and had to be held by other riders, and there were a few who were so badly wounded that they had to be tied across their saddles like sacks of grain, with their arms and legs dangling.

The leader of the riders, Niall, raised his hand and called the group to a halt when he spotted the wide-eyed, openmouthed children. Niall commanded the O'Byrne clan's small force of soldiers. The large man was pale, and there was a rough bandage tied around his head. One of his eyes was so bruised that it was almost shut.

"What happened?" Ronan asked in a whisper.

"The beast attacked us," Niall said, his voice harsh and croaking. "Come on now, this is no time to be playing in these woods—the thing may be after us. We have to reach the fort before dark."

"But what happened to the rest of the men?" Etan asked, as Niall gripped her arm and pulled her up onto the horse in front of him. "Where are they?"

"We are all that are left," Niall said sadly, looking back at the small group of warriors behind him. Etan counted the group; she thought there had been over twenty men that went out that morning, and now there were only ten. She stifled a gasp. Niall reached down and pulled Ronan up behind him. "Hold tight now," he said.

"But I thought you were going to kill the beast," Etan said in astonishment. "Father said that it didn't stand a chance."

"And you had some of the king's men with you also," Ronan added.

"I know," their uncle said wearily. "But we were wrong, and now there are eleven good men dead and devoured because of our mistake."

"What is Father going to say?" Ronan wondered as Niall raised his hand and nudged his horses into a trot.

Niall sighed and shook his head. "I wish I knew . . ."

Etan and Ronan's father, Dalbach, stood with his back to the huge roaring fire and listened silently to Niall's story. The large room was filled with people, mostly Dalbach's own warriors, but some from the High King's court at Tara. Servants moved around quietly, clearing the long table and filling the large cups with mead.

". . . and that's what happened," Niall finished. "We never had a chance. I've never seen anything move so fast in all my life." He took a quick swallow from the cup in his hand.

"Describe the creature," Dalbach said softly. He was a short, rather stout man, almost ten years older than his brother. His hair, which had once been as dark as his children's, was now thin and gray, and his thick, bushy beard was streaked with gray threads. There were lines on his forehead and under his eyes, and at this moment, he looked very old indeed.

"It was big," Niall said, "long and slender, with huge eyes . . ." He shook his head. "I can't remember anything else. It all happened so fast . . ."

Ronan and Etan pushed the door open very gently. They had been listening to Niall's tale through the door, but now they had to open it because their uncle's voice had grown so soft. They were both shivering in their long night robes, even though they had thrown heavy furs over their shoulders. They couldn't come into the warm room because they were supposed to be in bed.

"What's he saying?" Etan whispered in her brother's ear.

"*Shhh,* listen," he murmured.

". . . it all happened so fast," they heard Niall saying. "One moment the lake was smooth and calm, and the men were setting up their weapons, and the next thing we knew, the water just erupted up, and then this thing appeared." Niall shook his head. "It was terrible, terrible. We didn't stand a chance."

Dalbach nodded and then rested his hands on Niall's shoulders.

"What do we do now, sir?" someone in the room asked.

Dalbach straightened. "Well, we've tried force of arms. Now I'm afraid we must try magic."

A quick murmur ran around the room. The land of Erin was now Christian—there were some parts that still followed the old pagan faith, but magic was now frowned upon.

"I can't agree with that," said a rasping, harsh voice at the back of the room. All heads turned to look at the tall thin man in the simple brown robe of a monk.

"I don't agree with magic myself, Brother Colman," Dalbach said, "but I have no choice. There is an Oillpeist—a dragon-worm—living in a lake on my land. It has destroyed crops, uprooted trees, turned valuable land into waste ground, and lately it has started killing the animals. And now . . . well, you saw for yourself what it did today." Dalbach shook his head firmly. "I cannot allow it to go on."

"But there must be some other way," Brother Colman said, folding his arms and staring at the older man.

"Then tell me what it is and I will do it," Dalbach snapped. "No, Brother Colman, in this case there is nothing I can do."

"It is a sin," Brother Colman retorted.

"Probably," Dalbach murmured, and then he looked at one of the servants. "Bring the wise woman in."

"I cannot allow this," Brother Colman began.

"You cannot stop it," Niall growled.

"You—*you* are the king's man. You stop it," Brother

Colman said, turning to a hugely muscled man who was standing by the fire—Fergal, commander of the king's men. When Dalbach had asked for help, the king had sent him Fergal with a squad of men to help destroy the Oillpeist. But now three of his own men were dead, and over half of them wounded.

Fergal looked at Brother Colman with his ice-blue eyes, and then he slowly shook his head. "I would do exactly the same."

"Then I will tell the king," Brother Colman said loudly.

"And he will laugh at you," Fergal said with a smile. "He may follow the new faith, but he still has respect for the old ways."

Brother Colman opened his mouth to say something and then seemed to think better of it. He turned on his heel and walked toward the door.

Ronan and Etan saw him coming and had to make a dash for the shadows. They huddled together and held their breath as the door was flung open and a long bar of light was thrown out across the hall. Then Brother Colman stepped into the light and slammed the door shut behind him. The holy man's hard-soled sandals clattered down along the stone floor. At last they heard another door slam. With a sigh of relief, they darted back to the door and pressed their ears against the cold wood. They could hear their father speaking.

"This is Fand. She is the wise woman who has agreed to help us."

There was a dry cackling laugh, and then an almost rusty-sounding voice spoke. "I'm what that brown-robed one would call a witch. But he would only call me that because he's frightened of me. He forgets that his own St. Patrick used magic when he needed to."

Ronan and Etan pressed the door open again and peered in. They saw a small old woman sitting before the fire with her hands wrapped around a large cup of mead. She was dressed mostly in strips of animal furs, which had been sewn together into a huge shapeless dress, and there was a cloak that had also been made up out of animal skins thrown over her shoulders. Her face looked like an apple—an old dry wrinkled apple—but her eyes were bright and piercing. The two children couldn't make out the color of her eyes from the distance, although they did look to be a shade of red.

"We need your help, old woman," their father began.

"Oh, I know, I know," Fand cackled again, and both children were amazed to see that she still had all her own teeth.

"How do we get rid of the Oillpeist?" he asked.

"You feed it," Fand said, with another grin.

"Do you mean poison it?"

Fand laughed again, long and hard. Everyone there

felt shivers running up and down their spines at the eerie sound. "Yes, you might say that."

"If you tell me what sort of bait or poison you need, I can send to Tara for it," Fergal said.

The old woman took a drink from her cup. "Oh, I would imagine you would have the bait here."

"Well, what is it?" Dalbach asked impatiently.

"Watch," Fand said. She reached in under her cloak and then pulled out a small leather bag, which was held shut by a string pulled through the top. Holding the bag in one hand and the cup of mead in the other, she pulled it open with her teeth. Then she set it down on her knees and took out a tiny pinch of white powder.

"Watch," she said again, and then she threw the powder on the fire.

Everyone held their breath, expecting to see something happen—fire and sparks shooting around the room, or perhaps different-colored flames leaping high into the air. But nothing like that happened. People were just beginning to murmur among themselves when they noticed that the fire had gone very dull, and there seemed to be a lot more smoke than usual. But instead of drifting up into the chimney, this smoke hung in a solid mass just above the burning logs.

"Watch," Fand said for the third time, and colors began to coil and twist through the solid mass of gray smoke. The colors shifted and turned, bent and looped.

Soon the gray disappeared and was replaced by a shifting ball of light.

"Now look," the old woman said. All the shifting, twisting, coiling colors seemed to come together, and then a great gasp went around the room as a picture formed in the ball. It was an image of a small blue lake, surrounded by trees, with a bright blue sky and white clouds overhead. Birds darted across the sky, and the waters of the lake rippled in the breeze.

Everyone was watching the magic so closely that Ronan and Etan risked creeping into the room and hiding behind one of the tables that had been pushed into a corner. Now they could see everything clearly.

"I know that lake," Etan said, her breath tickling Ronan's ear.

He nodded. "So do I. It's the one we're not supposed to go near, the one where the Oillpeist lives."

His older sister nodded. Then she frowned. "What's that?" she asked, and her voice sounded so strange that Ronan quickly looked from her to the fire.

The image had grown, or perhaps they had somehow zoomed in on the lake, because they were now very close to the water's edge. They could see the burn and scorch marks on the earth, and the uprooted trees and seared bushes where the Oillpeist had crawled up out of the water. There was an old tree stump, too. The ragged stump had once been the children's favorite spot for sunbathing or fishing. It was perfectly flat and, even on the coolest day, it was always warm.

Now, however, it was burnt and blackened where the Oillpeist had breathed on it—but that was not what had upset his sister. It was Etan herself, tied to the ancient tree stump. In the magical image, she was dressed all in white and had a slim golden crown around her head. Her hair, which was usually tied up, was now loose and flowing down her back. She seemed to be sleeping.

Then the waters of the lake bubbled and boiled, and suddenly a huge head rose up through the mist, and two flat, slit-pupiled eyes swiveled to look at the girl. The massive head swooped . . . and the picture dissolved as a gust of wind blew through the room, disturbing the smoke.

Etan buried her head in her brother's shoulder to stop herself from screaming. Ronan could hear her heart thumping against his chest, and he knew his own pulse was racing, too. He wasn't sure what he had just seen or what it meant, but he had a very bad feeling about it.

"Would you care to explain this . . . this image?" Dalbach asked, his voice barely above a whisper.

"I would have thought you knew." Fand cackled. "To kill the Oillpeist, you must first feed it a young girl. A Christian girl should do very nicely." She paused and then added, "And of course, she must have some royal blood in her."

"But this is monstrous," Dalbach protested. "We cannot just sacrifice a human being to this creature."

Fand shrugged her bony shoulders. "All I know is that it never fails."

"Never?" Fergal asked, stepping forward from the fire.

"Never," Fand said.

Fergal turned back to Dalbach. "Well?" he asked.

"Well, what? Surely you don't expect me to . . ." He stopped when he saw the look in the warrior's eyes. "You do, don't you? You expect me to kill a young girl . . ."

"What will happen if the creature isn't destroyed?" Fergal asked the old woman.

"At the moment, the Oillpeist is still very small . . ."

"But it's *huge*!" Niall protested.

"It is still growing," Fand continued. "In another year or so it will be fully grown, and then . . ." She shrugged.

"And then?" Fergal asked.

Fand smiled. "And then it will be able to destroy this fort as easily as you or I crack an egg." The old woman began to laugh again, cackling and coughing until the tears streamed down her face. Some servants came in and took the old woman away, but everyone could still hear her shrill laughter echoing down along the corridors for a long time afterward.

"That girl in the picture," Fergal said at last, "who was she?"

Dalbach looked away. "I don't know," he said quickly.

Fergal eyed him. "I don't believe you," he said. "I was watching you when she appeared, aye, and Niall, too. You both know the girl—now who is she?"

"She is my daughter," Dalbach said eventually.

"She is a Christian? She has royal blood in her veins?"

Dalbach nodded miserably.

"Then she must be given to the Oillpeist."

"You'll have to kill me first," Dalbach snarled.

"If you do not send your daughter to the creature, I will ride to Tara and tell the king what has happened here. Then he will come here with an army; he will destroy your fort, make slaves of all your people, kill you and all your family and *then* send your daughter to the creature. So you have a choice . . ."

"A choice?" Dalbach shouted. "What choice do I have?"

Dalbach came to the children's room just before the sun rose the following morning. They were both awake— they hadn't slept all night—and were sitting up in bed waiting for him when he eased open the door and peeked inside. Dalbach was surprised to find them both awake at this early hour; usually they were almost impossible to get up in the morning.

"Oh, I didn't think you would be awake yet," he said softly, stepping into the room.

Etan and Ronan just looked at him.

"Something has happened," Dalbach said very slowly, "something terrible."

"We know, Father," Ronan said quietly. "We heard."

"But *how*?" he asked in astonishment.

"We were listening last night," Etan said. "We heard everything."

Dalbach sat down on the edge of Etan's bed and buried his head in his hands. "I don't want to do it," he said. His voice sounded rough and hoarse.

"I know," Etan whispered, although her own voice sounded tight, and her throat was burning.

"But I've got no choice," Dalbach continued. "If we don't kill the Oillpeist, then it will ravage the country. If I don't give you to the creature, then the High King will come with his army and destroy us, and then he will give you to the Oillpeist anyway. What do I do?"

Dalbach sounded so lost and lonely that Etan rested her head against his back and wrapped her arms around his shoulders. Ronan got up out of his bed and knelt on the floor beside his father. "Don't worry," he whispered. "We've got a plan."

"When . . . when do I go to the Oillpeist?" Etan asked slowly.

Dalbach stood up and looked at both his children. His eyes were bright and shining, and he seemed to have aged many years in the single night. "This morning; you go to the creature this morning," he whispered. Then he turned and hurried from the room.

A sad, silent procession wound its way down along the white path that led into the forest and the lake. Dalbach and Niall rode at the front, with Ronan and Etan behind them on their own small ponies. Behind them came Fergal with the rest of the warriors, and behind these, most of the servants from the fort. No one said anything and even the sounds of the forest—the chirpings of the birds, the crackling of the leaves and branches as the smaller animals pushed their way through the undergrowth—seemed to be missing. Everyone was still and waiting.

Etan was dressed exactly as she had been in Fand's magical moving image. She was wearing a long white robe of the finest material, with an ancient Celtic pattern in rich gold thread running along the hem, the neck, and the cuffs of the sleeves. There was a simple golden metal band resting on her rich dark hair, which, this morning, had been brushed until it shone and flowed down her back. Etan was pale, and her eyes were red-rimmed, but she rode her pony with her head held high.

Ronan trotted his animal along beside her. He and his sister had often fought—what brother and sister didn't?—but he admired her now. She was so calm, and yet she knew she was almost certainly going to her death in the jaws of a terrible creature.

Soon the trees thinned out and the riders spotted the blue water of the lake. The path led downward and twisted around two huge trees, out onto a rough stony shore. Here everyone stopped and stared at the lake.

The lake was not large, but it was supposed to be bottomless. A deep underground river connected it to another lake farther west, which, in turn, led down to the sea. The water itself was very dark and dirty-looking; all the land around the lake was bog-land, and the peat seeped into the water, coloring it. It was exactly the sort of lake an Oillpeist would choose to live in.

"Quickly now," Fergal said, riding up behind Dalbach, Etan, and Ronan. "We don't have much time. Where's the tree stump we saw last night?"

Ronan pointed off to one side, where a clump of trees and bushes came down almost to the water's edge. They were crushed and burnt, and the earth all around them was torn and scarred, as if some huge beast had pulled itself up by its claws.

Dalbach looked at his daughter. "You don't have to go, you know that?" he whispered. "I'll fight for you— I'd fight the High King for you."

"But the Oillpeist is still growing," Etan whispered. "What will happen in a few years' time when it is destroying the countryside? I can stop it."

Dalbach kissed his daughter on the forehead. "Your

mother would have been very proud of you," he whispered. The children's mother, Almu, had died when Ronan had been only a few days old. Everyone said she was a lovely, kind woman, whom Etan resembled.

Fergal then took Etan by the hand and walked her down to the edge of the water and the tree stump. He produced a length of rope and quickly looped it around her waist and then onto the scorched tree stump.

"It's not very tight," Etan said.

Fergal smiled sadly. "I know you must think very badly of me," he said. "I have a daughter of my own about your age, too. But you know it has to be done, don't you?"

Etan nodded.

Fergal finished tying the knot, stepped back, and pulled his sword free, saluting Etan as if she were a queen. "You are a very brave young lady," he said quietly, and then he stepped back from the tree stump and marched up the beach.

"What do we do now?" Dalbach asked, hardly able to look at the small figure of his daughter tied to the blackened tree stump by the water's edge.

"Now we wait," Fergal said.

They waited on into the morning, but nothing happened. The sun rose in the heavens and crept across the sky, and the shadows on the ground grew shorter and shorter, until they had almost disappeared . . .

At exactly midday, the Oillpeist appeared.

At first there was just an undulation on the surface of the water—a simple ripple, as if a stone had been dropped in. And then the ripple grew and grew, spreading out from the center of the lake in ever-growing circles. Large bubbles appeared on the surface of the lake. These bubbles burst with quick, sharp pops, leaving a foul odor on the air.

The water in the center of the lake began to boil, frothing yellow-white. Then a head appeared.

The Oillpeist.

The head was long and flat, with two huge catlike eyes set on either side of a bony ridge that ran down the center of its face and formed a birdlike beak. Its body was long and covered with hard black scales. It had six legs, each one ending in three massive talons, and a tail that broke the surface of the water and waved in the air, studded with spiky bones.

The Oillpeist's evil-looking head waved to and fro, as if it were looking for something. Two tendrils of gray smoke drifted from its nostrils. Suddenly it spotted Etan. It swooped . . .

. . . and stopped before her, its huge eyes wide and unblinking, and the tip of a forked tongue flickering between its lips.

Etan pulled as far away from the creature as possible, but, although Fergal had tied her loosely, she was still secure. She turned her head away and took a deep breath—the smell was terrible.

The Oillpeist lifted its huge head, opened its mouth, and roared. The sound was so powerful that it knocked everyone to the ground; horses reared up and galloped off into the forest, and the lake was churned to a frenzy. A huge spout of flame shot out from the Oillpeist and curled into the air.

And then the Oillpeist twisted its head toward her and it opened its huge mouth . . .

Etan saw its rows of massive yellowed teeth, and its long black tongue in its raw red mouth, and she squeezed her eyes shut and said a final prayer . . .

Someone moved in the bushes by her side.

It was Ronan.

With a scream that was almost as terrifying as the Oillpeist's, he dashed from his hiding place, swinging something over his head. It sailed through the air, straight down the creature's throat . . .

The Oillpeist closed his mouth with surprise, and then it opened it with a roar and spit flame at him. Smoke trickled out, and then there was a muffled *whump* as the Oillpeist's head was engulfed in flame. It reared up, screaming, as the flames burned through it. Now there were flames coming from its mouth and nose and ears. It thrashed its head around, trying to shake off the fire, but it was too late. With a final scream, the Oillpeist slumped down onto the stony beach by Etan's feet. It was dead.

The girl opened one eye and then looked at her brother. "It worked," she said with a sigh of relief.

"Of course it worked! I told you it would."

"But you might have been wrong," Etan said with a smile, "and then what would have happened to me?"

Dalbach came running up. He fell to his knees and hugged his two children. "What did you throw at it?" he finally asked Ronan.

The boy smiled. "A jug of fish oil."

The Oillpeist usually spat out a long streamer of flame, but when it had bitten down on the jug Ronan had thrown into its mouth, the oil had spread everywhere. When the Oillpeist had spat fire again, the inside of its mouth had been engulfed in flame!

Ronan and Etan were heroes. She had been willing to sacrifice herself to save Erin, and he had defeated the Oillpeist where everyone else had failed. And though the two children never did any other heroic deeds, people still remembered the heroes who saved Ireland with self-sacrifice and a jug of fish oil.

Acknowledgments

This book, and its companion volume, would not have happened without the constant support and encouragement (and endless patience) of Beverly Horowitz and Hannah Hill at Delacorte Press/Random House.

Special thanks also to Krista Marino and Colleen Fellingham (who has kept me safe and out of trouble these many years).

Thank you, as always, to Barry Krost and Melanie Rose at Barry Krost Management, who do all the real work.

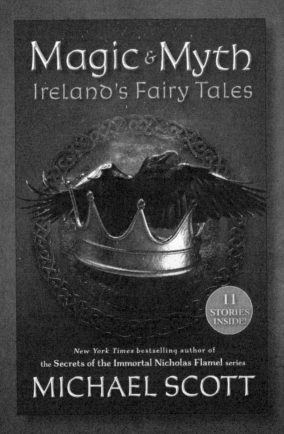

Keep reading for a peek at the first book in

THE SECRETS OF THE IMMORTAL NICHOLAS FLAMEL SERIES!

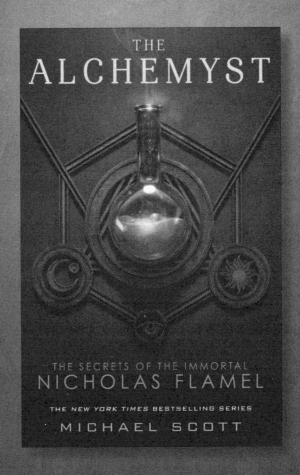

CHAPTER ONE

"*OK*—answer me this: why would anyone want to wear an overcoat in San Francisco in the middle of summer?" Sophie Newman pressed her fingers against the Bluetooth earpiece as she spoke.

On the other side of the continent, her fashion-conscious friend Elle inquired matter-of-factly, "What sort of coat?"

Wiping her hands on the cloth tucked into her apron strings, Sophie moved out from behind the counter of the empty coffee shop and stepped up to the window, watching men emerge from the car across the street. "Heavy black wool overcoats. They're even wearing black gloves and hats. And sunglasses." She pressed her face against the glass. "Even for this city, that's just a little *too* weird."

"Maybe they're undertakers?" Elle suggested, her voice popping and clicking on the cell phone. Sophie could hear something loud and dismal playing in the background— Lacrimosa maybe, or Amorphis. Elle had never quite got over her Goth phase.

"Maybe," Sophie answered, sounding unconvinced. She'd been chatting on the phone with her friend when, a few moments earlier, she'd spotted the unusual-looking car. It was long and sleek and looked as if it belonged in an old black-and-white movie. As it drove past the window, sunlight reflected off the blacked-out windows, briefly illuminating the interior of the coffee shop in warm yellow-gold light, blinding Sophie. Blinking away the black spots dancing before her eyes, she watched as the car turned at the bottom of the hill and slowly returned. Without signaling, it pulled over directly in front of The Small Book Shop, right across the street.

"Maybe they're Mafia," Elle suggested dramatically. "My dad knows someone in the Mafia. But he drives a Prius," she added.

"This is most definitely not a Prius," Sophie said, looking again at the car and the two large men standing on the street bundled up in their heavy overcoats, gloves and hats, their eyes hidden behind overlarge sunglasses.

"Maybe they're just cold," Elle suggested. "Doesn't it get cool in San Francisco?"

Sophie Newman glanced at the clock and thermometer on the wall over the counter behind her. "It's two-fifteen here . . . and eighty-one degrees," she said. "Trust me, they're not cold. They must be dying. Wait," she said, interrupting herself, "something's happening."

The rear door opened and another man, even larger than

the first two, climbed stiffly out of the car. As he closed the door, sunlight briefly touched his face and Sophie caught a glimpse of pale, unhealthy-looking gray-white skin. She adjusted the volume on the earpiece. "OK. You should see what just climbed out of the car. A huge guy with gray skin. Gray. That might explain it; maybe they have some type of skin condition."

"I saw a National Geographic documentary about people who can't go out in the sun . . . ," Elle began, but Sophie was no longer listening to her.

A fourth figure stepped out of the car.

He was a small, rather dapper-looking man, dressed in a neat charcoal-gray three-piece suit that looked vaguely old-fashioned but that she could tell had been tailor-made for him. His iron-gray hair was pulled back from an angular face into a tight ponytail, while a neat triangular beard, mostly black but flecked with gray, concealed his mouth and chin. He moved away from the car and stepped under the striped awning that covered the trays of books outside the shop. When he picked up a brightly colored paperback and turned it over in his hands, Sophie noticed that he was wearing gray gloves. A pearl button at the wrist winked in the light.

"They're going into the bookshop," she said into her earpiece.

"Is Josh still working there?" Elle immediately asked.

Sophie ignored the sudden interest in her friend's voice. The fact that her best friend liked her twin brother was just a little too weird. "Yeah. I'm going to call him to see what's up. I'll call you right back." She hung up, pulled out the earpiece and absently rubbed her hot ear as she stared, fascinated, at the small man. There was something about him . . . something *odd*. Maybe he was a fashion designer, she thought, or a movie producer, or maybe he was an author—she'd noticed that some authors liked to dress up in peculiar outfits. She'd give him a few minutes to get into the shop, then she'd call her twin for a report.

Sophie was about to turn away when the gray man suddenly spun around and seemed to stare directly at her. As he stood under the awning, his face was in shadow, and yet for just the briefest instant, his eyes looked as if they were glowing.

Sophie knew—*just knew*—that there was no possible way for the small gray man to see her: she was standing on the opposite side of the street behind a pane of glass that was bright with reflected early-afternoon sunlight. She would be invisible in the gloom behind the glass.

And yet . . .

And yet in that single moment when their eyes met, Sophie felt the tiny hairs on the back of her hands and along her forearms tingle and felt a puff of cold air touch the back of her neck. She rolled her shoulders, turning her head slightly from side to side, strands of her long blond hair curling across her cheek. The contact lasted only a second before the small man looked away, but Sophie got the impression that he had looked directly at her.

In the instant before the gray man and his three overdressed companions disappeared into the bookshop, Sophie decided that she did not like him.

✧   ✧   ✧

Peppermint.

And rotten eggs.

"That is just vile." Josh Newman stood in the center of the bookstore's cellar and breathed deeply. Where *were* those smells coming from? He looked around at the shelves stacked high with books and wondered if something had crawled in behind them and died. What else would account for such a foul stink? The tiny cramped cellar always smelled dry and musty, the air heavy with the odors of parched curling paper, mingled with the richer aroma of old leather bindings and dusty cobwebs. He loved the smell; he always thought it was warm and comforting, like the scents of cinnamon and spices that he associated with Christmas.

Peppermint.

Sharp and clean, the smell cut through the close cellar atmosphere. It was the odor of new toothpaste or those herbal teas his sister served in the coffee shop across the street. It sliced through the heavier smells of leather and paper, and was so strong that it made his sinuses tingle; he felt as if he was going to sneeze at any moment. He quickly pulled out his iPod earbuds. Sneezing with headphones on was not a good idea: made your ears pop.

Eggs.

Foul and stinking—he recognized the sulfurous odor of rotten eggs. It blanketed the clear odor of mint . . . and it was disgusting. He could feel the stench coating his tongue and lips, and his scalp began to itch as if something were crawling through it. Josh ran his fingers through his shaggy blond hair and shuddered. The drains must be backing up.

Leaving the earbuds dangling over his shoulders, he checked the book list in his hand, then looked at the shelves again: *The Complete Works of Charles Dickens,* twenty-seven volumes, red leather binding. Now where was he going to find that?

Josh had been working in the bookshop for nearly two months and still didn't have the faintest idea where anything was. There was no filing system . . . or rather, there *was* a system, but it was known only to Nick and Perry Fleming, the owners of The Small Book Shop. Nick or his wife could put their hands on any book in either the shop upstairs or the cellar in a matter of minutes.

A wave of peppermint, immediately followed by rotten eggs, filled the air again; Josh coughed and felt his eyes water. This was impossible! Stuffing the book list into one pocket of his jeans and the headphones into the other, he maneuvered his way through the piled books and stacks of boxes, heading for the stairs. He couldn't spend another minute down there with the smell. He rubbed the heels of his palms against his eyes, which were now stinging furiously. Grabbing the stair rail, he pulled himself up. He needed a breath of fresh air or he was going to throw up—but, strangely, the closer he came to the top of the stairs, the stronger the odors became.

He popped his head out of the cellar door and looked around.

And in that instant, Josh Newman realized that the world would never be the same again.

CHAPTER TWO

*J*osh peered over the edge of the cellar, eyes watering with the stink of sulfur and mint. His first impression was that the usually quiet shop was crowded: four men facing Nick Fleming, the owner, three of them huge and hulking, one smaller and sinister-looking. Josh immediately guessed that the shop was being robbed.

His boss, Nick Fleming, stood in the middle of the bookshop, facing the others. He was a rather ordinary-looking man. Average height and build, with no real distinguishing features, except for his eyes, which were so pale that they were almost completely colorless. His black hair was cropped close to his skull and he always seemed to have stubble on his chin, as if he hadn't shaved for a couple of days. He was dressed as usual in simple black jeans, a loose black T-shirt advertising a concert that had taken place twenty-five years earlier, and a pair of battered cowboy boots. There was a cheap digital watch on his left wrist and a heavy silver-link bracelet on his right, alongside two tatty multicolored friendship bracelets.

Facing him was a small gray man in a smart suit.

Josh realized that they were not speaking . . . and yet something was going on between them. Both men were standing still, their arms close to their bodies, elbows tucked in, open palms turned upward. Nick was in the center of the shop, while the gray man was standing close to the door, his three black-coated companions around him. Strangely, both men's fingers were moving, twitching, dancing, as if they were typing furiously, thumb brushing against forefinger, little finger touching thumb, index and little finger extended. Tendrils and wisps of green mist gathered in Fleming's palms, then curled in ornate patterns and drifted onto the floor, where they writhed like serpents. Foul, yellow-tinged smoke coiled and dripped from the gray man's gloved hands, spattering onto the wooden floor like dirty liquid.

The stench rolled off the smoke, thickening the atmosphere with the scent of peppermint and sulfur. Josh felt his stomach twist and lurch and he swallowed hard; the rotten-egg smell was enough to make him gag.

The air between the two men shimmered with tendrils of green and yellow smoke, and where they touched, sparks hissed and sizzled. Fleming's fingers moved, and a long fist-thick coil of green smoke appeared in the palm of his hand. He blew on it, a quick hissing breath, and it spun up into the air, twisting and untwisting at head height between the two men. The gray man's short, stubby fingers tapped out their own rhythm and a yellow ball of energy spun from his hands and bobbed away. It touched the coil of green smoke, which immediately wrapped around the ball. There was a sparking *snap* . . . and the invisible explosion blew both men backward across the room, sending them crashing across the tables of books. Lightbulbs popped and fluorescents shattered, raining powdery glass onto the floor. Two of the windows exploded outward, while another dozen of the small square panes shattered and spiderwebbed.

Nick Fleming tumbled to the floor, close to the opening to the cellar, almost landing on top of Josh, who was standing frozen on the steps, wide-eyed with shock and horror. As Nick clambered to his feet, he pushed Josh back down the stairs. "Stay down, whatever happens, stay down," he hissed, his English touched with an indefinable accent. He straightened as he turned and Josh saw him turn his right palm upward, bring it close to his face and blow into it. Then he made a throwing motion toward the center of the room, as if he were lobbing a ball.

Josh craned his neck to follow the movement. But there was nothing to see . . . and then it was as if all the air had been sucked out of the room. Books were suddenly ripped from the nearby shelves, drawn into an untidy heap in the center of the floor; framed prints were dragged from the walls; a heavy woolen rug curled upward and was sucked into the center of the room.

Then the heap exploded.

Two of the big men in black overcoats caught the full force of the explosion. Josh watched as books, some heavy and hard, others soft and sharp, flew around them like angry birds. He winced in sympathy as one man took the full force of a dictionary in the face. It knocked away his hat and sunglasses . . . revealing dead-looking, muddy, gray skin and eyes like polished black stones. A shelf of romance novels battered against his companion's face, snapping the cheap sunglasses in two. Josh discovered that he, too, had eyes that looked like stones.

And he suddenly realized that they *were* stones.

He was turning to Nick Fleming, a question forming on his lips, when his boss glanced at him. "Stay down," he commanded. "He's brought Golems." Fleming ducked as the gray man sent three long spearlike blades of yellow energy across the room. They sliced through bookshelves and stabbed into the wooden floor. Everything they touched immediately started to rot and putrefy. Leather bindings snapped and cracked, paper blackened, wooden floorboards and shelves turned dry and powdery.

Fleming tossed another invisible ball into the corner of the room. Josh Newman followed the motion of his boss's arm. As the unseen ball sailed through the air, a shaft of sunlight caught it, and for an instant, he saw it glow green and faceted, like an emerald globe. Then it moved out of the sunlight and vanished again. This time when it hit the floor, the effect was even more dramatic. There was no sound, but the entire building shook. Tables of cheap paperbacks dissolved into matchwood, and slivers of paper filled the air with bizarre confetti. Two of the men in black—the Golems—were slammed back against the shelves, bringing books tumbling down on top of them, while a third—the biggest—was pushed so hard against the door that he was propelled out onto the street.

And in the silence that followed came the sound of gloved hands clapping. "You have perfected that technique, I see, Nicholas." The gray man spoke English with a curious lilt.

"I've been practicing, John," Nick Fleming said, sliding toward the open cellar door, shoving Josh Newman farther down the stairs. "I knew you would catch up with me sooner or later."

"We've been looking for you for a very long time, Nicholas. You've got something of ours. And we want it back."

A sliver of yellow smoke bit into the ceiling above Fleming's and Josh's heads. Bubbling, rotten black plaster drifted down like bitter snowflakes.

"I burned it," Fleming said, "burned it a long time ago." He pushed Josh even farther into the cellar, then pulled the sliding door closed, sealing them both in. "Don't ask," he warned, his pale eyes shining in the gloom. "Not now." Catching Josh by the arm, Nick pulled him into the darkest corner of the bookstore cellar, caught a section of shelving in both hands and jerked it forward. There was a click, and the shelving swung outward, revealing a set of steps hidden behind it. Fleming urged Josh forward into the gloom. "Quickly now, quickly and quietly," he warned. He followed Josh into the opening and pulled the shelves closed behind him just as the cellar door turned into a foul black liquid and flowed down the stairs with the most appalling stench of sulfur.

"Up." Nick Fleming's voice was warm against Josh's ear. "This comes out in the empty shop next door to ours. We have to hurry. It'll take Dee only a few moments to realize what's happened."

Josh Newman nodded; he knew the shop. The dry cleaner's had been empty all summer. He had a hundred questions, and none of the answers that ran through his mind was satisfactory, since most of them contained that one awful word in them: *magic*. He had just watched two men toss balls and spears of something—of *energy*—at each other. He had witnessed the destruction those energies had caused.

Josh had just witnessed magic.

But of course, everyone knew that magic simply did not and could not exist.

About the Author

An authority on mythology and folklore, Michael Scott is one of Ireland's most successful authors. A master of fantasy, science fiction, and horror, he was hailed by the *Irish Times* as "the King of Fantasy in these isles." Look for the six books in his New York Times bestselling The Secrets of the Immortal Nicholas Flamel series: *The Alchemyst, The Magician, The Sorceress, The Necromancer, The Warlock,* and *The Enchantress.* You can visit Michael Scott at dillonscott.com and follow him on Facebook and Twitter.